GREG HILDEBRANDT'S

MAGICAL STORYBOOK TREASURY

THE WONDERFUL WIZARD OF OZ
by L. Frank Baum

THE ADVENTURES OF PINOCCHIO
by Carlo Collodi

ALICE'S ADVENTURES IN WONDERLAND
by Lewis Carroll

COURAGE
BOOKS
AN IMPRINT OF RUNNING PRESS
PHILADELPHIA • LONDON

TABLE
OF
CONTENTS

The
Wonderful
Wizard
of
OZ

by L. Frank Baum

Illustrated by Greg Hildebrandt

orothy lived on the great Kansas prairies with her Uncle Henry and Aunt Em. Their house was only one room. There was no attic and the only cellar was a small hole in the ground called a cyclone cellar, where the family could go in case a great whirlwind arose.

Gray prairie surrounded the gray house. Aunt Em and Uncle Henry were gray as well. It was Toto, a little black dog with long silky hair, who saved Dorothy from growing as gray as her other surroundings. Dorothy played with him and loved him dearly.

Today they were not playing. Uncle Henry looked anxiously at the sky, which was more gray than usual. Dorothy was looking at the sky too. Aunt Em was washing dishes. A cyclone was coming. Uncle Henry went to the sheds to look after the cows and horses.

Aunt Em dropped her work and came to the door. One glance told her the cyclone was close. "Quick Dorothy!" she screamed. "Run for the cellar!"

Toto ran under the bed, and Dorothy tried to get him. Aunt Em, badly frightened, threw open the trap door in the floor and climbed down into the cellar. Dorothy caught Toto at last and started to follow her aunt. When she was halfway across the room there came a great shriek of wind, and the house shook so hard that she fell to the floor.

Then a strange thing happened. The house whirled around two or three times and rose slowly through the air until it was caught up and carried by the cyclone for many miles.

It was very dark and the wind howled horribly around her, but Dorothy found she was riding quite easily.

Toto ran about the room, barking loudly; but Dorothy sat quite still on the floor and waited to see what would happen. Finally she crawled to her bed and fell asleep.

Dorothy was awakened suddenly and sat up. The house was not moving. Bright sunshine came in the window and she ran to the door to look outside.

The country outside was beautiful, with patches of bright green grass, trees bearing rich and luscious fruits, and gorgeous flowers. Unusual and beautiful birds flew by, while a small brook sparkled.

Dorothy noticed an odd group of people coming toward her. They seemed about as tall as her, but they looked many years older. Three were men and one a woman, all oddly dressed. They wore round hats that rose to a small point a foot above their heads, with little bells around the brims that tinkled. The men wore all blue, while the woman wore a white gown that glistened like diamonds. The men, Dorothy thought, were about as old as Uncle Henry, for two of them had beards. But the little woman was much older.

Seeing Dorothy, they paused and whispered amongst themselves, as if afraid to come farther. But the little old woman walked up to Dorothy, made a low bow and said in a sweet voice:

"You are welcome, most noble Sorceress, to the land of the Munchkins. They are so grateful to you for having killed the Wicked Witch of the East, and for setting their people free from slavery to her."

The old woman pointed to the corner of Dorothy's house. Dorothy looked, and gave a little cry of fright. There, indeed, were two feet sticking out from under the house, shod in silver shoes with pointed toes.

"I am the Munchkins' friend, the Good Witch of the North. There is another Good Witch, in the South. Those who dwelt in the East and the West were, indeed, wicked witches. Now that you have killed one of them, there is but one Wicked Witch in all the Land of Oz—the one who lives in the West."

Just then the Munchkins, who had been standing silently by, gave a loud shout and pointed to the corner of the house where the Wicked Witch had been lying. The feet of the dead Witch had disappeared entirely, and nothing was left but the silver shoes.

The Wicked Witch of the East had dried up in the sun, but the silver shoes were still left.

The Good Witch handed them to Dorothy to keep.

"The Witch of the East was proud of those Silver Shoes," said one of the Munchkins, "and there is some charm connected with them; but what it is we never knew."

Dorothy asked the Munchkins if they could help her find her way back to Kansas.

The Munchkins and the Witch shook their heads.

"You must go to the Emerald City. Perhaps the Great Wizard Oz will help you," said the Good Witch of the North.

"Where is this city?" asked Dorothy.

"It is exactly in the center of the country, and is ruled by Oz, the Great Wizard."

"Is he a good man?" inquired the girl anxiously.

"He is a good Wizard. Whether he is a man or not I cannot tell, for I have never seen him."

"How can I get there?" asked Dorothy.

"You must walk. It is a long journey, through a country that is sometimes pleasant and sometimes dangerous. However, I will use all the magic I know of to keep you from harm. I will give you my kiss as protection, and no one will dare injure you," said the Good Witch of the North.

She came close to Dorothy and kissed her gently on the forehead. Then she pointed to the road to the Emerald City, which was paved with yellow bricks, said goodbye, and disappeared. The Munchkins wished Dorothy well, and departed through the trees.

Dorothy put on her blue and white checked gingham dress and pink sun-bonnet, filled a little basket with bread, and put on the Silver Shoes that had belonged to the Witch of the East.

She started down the road paved with yellow bricks. Around her were neat fences painted a dainty blue, fields of grain and vegetables in abundance, and once in a while a house that was round with a big dome roof. All the houses were painted blue, for in this country of the East, blue was the favorite color.

The people came out to look at her and bow low as she went by; for everyone knew she had destroyed the Wicked Witch of the East and set them free from bondage.

Toward evening, Dorothy came to a large Munchkin house, where men and women were dancing and singing to celebrate their freedom from the bondage of the Wicked Witch.

Dorothy ate a hearty supper and was waited upon by the rich Munchkin, Boq. She sat and watched the people dance, then slept soundly in the house until morning.

Dorothy bade her friends good-bye and started again down the yellow brick road. When she had gone several miles she stopped to rest, sitting on a fence beside the road. Not far away a Scarecrow in an old blue Munchkin suit was placed high on a pole in the middle of a field, to keep birds away from the ripe corn.

Dorothy gazed at the Scarecrow. Suddenly, the Scarecrow slowly winked at her. She thought she must have been mistaken at first, for none of the scarecrows in Kansas ever wink; but presently the figure nodded its head to her in a friendly way. She went up to the Scarecrow.

"Good day," said the Scarecrow.

"Did you speak?" asked the girl, in wonder.

"Certainly," answered the Scarecrow. "How do you do?"

"I'm pretty well, thank you," replied Dorothy politely. "How do you do?"

"I'm not feeling well," said the Scarecrow, with a smile, "for it is very tedious being perched up here night and day to scare away crows. If you will please take away the pole which is stuck up my back I shall be greatly obliged to you."

Dorothy lifted the figure off the pole for, being stuffed with straw, it was quite light.

"Thank you very much," said the Scarecrow. "Who are you? And where are you going?"

"My name is Dorothy," said the girl, "and I am going to the Emerald City, to ask the Great Oz to send me back home."

"Do you think," the Scarecrow asked, "that Oz would give me some brains?" For he was stuffed, and had no brains.

"If you will come with me, I'll ask Oz to do all he can for you," Dorothy replied.

"Thank you," he answered gratefully.

They walked back to the road. After a while they came to a dark forest. Suddenly there was a deep groan nearby. A man, made entirely of tin, was standing beside a tree that was partially chopped through, an uplifted axe in his hands.

"Did you groan?" asked Dorothy.

"Yes," answered the tin man, "I did. I've been groaning for more than a year, and no one has ever heard me before or come to help me. Please get an oil can from my cottage and oil my joints. They are rusted so badly that I cannot move them at all; if I am well-oiled I shall soon be all right again."

Dorothy ran into the cottage and found the oil can, then she returned and oiled all of the man's joints.

The Tin Woodman gave a sigh of satisfaction and lowered his axe.

"This is a great comfort," he said. "I have been holding that axe in the air ever since I rusted, and I'm glad to be able to put it down at last. I might have

stood there always if you had not come along," he said; "so you have certainly saved my life. How did you happen to be here?"

"We are on our way to the Emerald City to see the Great Oz," she answered.

"Why do you wish to see Oz?" he asked.

"I want him to send me back to Kansas, and the Scarecrow wants him to put a few brains into his head," she replied.

The Tin Woodman appeared to think deeply for a moment. Then he said:

"Do you suppose Oz could give me a heart?"

"Why, I guess so," Dorothy answered. "It would be as easy as to give the Scarecrow brains."

"True," the Tin Woodman returned. "So, if you will allow me to join your party, I will also go to the Emerald City and ask Oz to help me."

"Come along," said the Scarecrow heartily, and Dorothy added that she would be pleased to have his company.

The Tin Woodman had asked Dorothy to put the oil can in her basket. "For," he said, "if I should get caught in the rain and rust again, I would need the oil can badly."

The travelers continued on the yellow brick road. Suddenly, from the woods there came a terrible roar, and the next moment a great Lion bounded into the road. With one blow of his paw he sent the Scarecrow spinning over and over to the edge of the road, and then he struck at the Tin Woodman with his sharp claws. But, to the Lion's surprise, he could make no impression on the tin, although the Woodman fell over in the road and lay still.

Little Toto, now that he had an enemy to face, ran barking toward the Lion, and the great beast had opened his mouth to bite the dog, when Dorothy rushed forward and slapped the Lion upon his nose as hard as she could, while she cried out:

"Don't you dare bite Toto!"

"I didn't bite him," said the Lion, rubbing his nose where Dorothy had hit him.

"No, but you tried to," she retorted. "You are nothing but a big coward."

"I know it," said the Lion, hanging his head in shame. "I've always known it. But how can I help it?"

"Come with us to see Oz, and he will give you courage," said Dorothy.

"Then, if you don't mind, I'll go with you," said the Lion, "for my life is simply unbearable without a bit of courage."

"You will be very welcome," answered Dorothy, "for you will help to keep away the other wild beasts."

So once more the little company set off upon their journey.

After a while the forest grew very thick, dark, and gloomy. Strange noises came from the depths of the forest.

The travelers came upon a deep gulf across the road. The Tin Woodman chopped down a large tree, so that they could cross the gulf. They had just started to cross the tree-bridge when a sharp growl made them all look up, and to their horror they saw running toward them two great beasts with bodies like bears and heads like tigers.

"They are the Kalidahs!" said the Cowardly Lion, beginning to tremble.

Dorothy grabbed Toto and crossed the bridge. The Scarecrow and the Tin Woodman followed. The Lion crossed the bridge, then turned to roar at the Kalidahs, who paused, but seeing they were bigger than him, and remembering that there were two of them and only one of the Lion, the Kalidahs again rushed forward.

The Tin Woodman began to chop the tree at once, and, just as the two Kalidahs were nearly across, the tree fell with a crash into the gulf, carrying the ugly, snarling brutes with it, and both were dashed to pieces on the sharp rocks at the bottom.

This adventure made the travelers more anxious than ever to get out of the forest. They walked quickly, and finally came upon a swiftly flowing river. The Tin Woodman took his axe and began to chop down small trees to make a raft. When the raft was finished, the four travelers got on. They got along quite well at first, but when they reached the middle of the river the swift current swept the raft downstream, farther and farther away from the road of yellow brick. The water grew so deep that the long poles the Tin Woodman and the Scarecrow were using to push the raft could not touch the bottom.

"This is bad," said the Tin Woodman, "for if we cannot get to land, we shall be carried into the country of the Wicked Witch of the West, and she will enchant us and make us her slaves."

"We must certainly get to the Emerald City if we can," the Scarecrow said, and he pushed so hard on his long pole that it stuck fast in the mud at the bottom of the river. Then, before he could pull it out again or let go, the raft was swept away, and the poor Scarecrow was left clinging to the pole in the middle of the river.

The Lion sprang into the water, and the Tin Woodman caught hold of his tail. Then the Lion swam toward the shore. Upon reaching the shore, the travelers made their way back to the Scarecrow, still stuck in the middle of the river.

Just then a Stork flew by, who saved the Scarecrow from the river. The Scarecrow was much obliged.

When the Scarecrow found himself among his friends again, he was so happy that he hugged them all. "Thank you," Dorothy told the Stork, and then the kind Stork flew into the air and was soon out of sight.

The travelers walked along until they came to a large field of scarlet poppies, whose odor makes anyone who breathes it fall asleep. If the sleeper is not carried away from the scent of the flowers, he sleeps on and on forever. Presently Dorothy fell asleep.

"What shall we do?" asked the Tin Woodman.

"If we leave her here she will die," said the Lion. "The smell of the flowers is killing us all. I myself can scarcely keep my eyes open. I will run fast, and try to reach the edge of the field."

Toto and Dorothy were asleep, but the Scarecrow and Tin Woodman, not being made of flesh, were not troubled by the scent of the flowers. The Scarecrow and Tin Woodman picked up Toto and put the dog in Dorothy's lap and carried her. It seemed that the great carpet of deadly flowers would never end. At last, they came upon the Lion, fast asleep among the poppies only a short distance from the end of the poppy bed. Beyond it lay green grassy fields.

"We can do nothing for him," said the Tin Woodman, sadly, "for he is much

too heavy to lift. We must leave him here to sleep on forever, and perhaps he will dream that he has found courage at last."

They carried Dorothy and Toto farther, and laid them gently on the ground, far away from the deadly smell of the poppies. Suddenly, the woodman heard a low growl, and saw a great yellow wildcat chasing a little gray field mouse. The cat's mouth was wide open, showing two rows of sharp teeth. Its eyes were red. Even though he had no heart the Woodman knew it was wrong to kill such a pretty, helpless creature. Raising his axe, he chopped the wildcat's head off.

The field mouse, now that it was safe from its enemy, drew near and said, in a squeaky little voice:

"Oh thank you ever so much for saving my life. I am the Queen of the Field Mice. Let my subjects repay your brave deed by granting you a wish."

The Tin Woodman and the Scarecrow wished for the mice to save their friend the Cowardly Lion. The Queen sent for all her subjects to come with a piece of string, to pull the Cowardly Lion out of the poppy field on a cart that the Tin Woodman made out of tree branches.

The mice were harnessed to the cart, and with the Woodman and the Scarecrow pushing from behind, soon the Lion was out of the poppy field. Dorothy awoke and thanked the little mice warmly for saving her companion from death.

Then the mice were unharnessed from the cart and scampered away through the grass to their homes. The Queen of the Mice was the last to leave.

"If ever you need us again," she said, "come out into the field and call, and we shall hear you and come to your assistance. Good-bye!"

"Good-bye!" they all answered, and away the Queen ran.

After this they sat down beside the Lion until he should awaken.

The Cowardly Lion awoke after awhile, and was very glad to find himself still alive.

When the Lion was feeling quite himself again, they all started down the yellow brick road. The country was beautiful. The fences and houses beside the road were painted green. The people dressed in a lovely emerald-green color and wore peaked hats like those of the Munchkins.

"This must be the Land of Oz," said Dorothy, "and we are surely getting near the Emerald City."

Soon there was a beautiful green glow in the sky just before them.

As they walked on, the green glow became brighter. By afternoon they came to the great wall that surrounded the City. It was high and thick and of a bright green color.

In front of them was a big gate, studded with emeralds that glittered in the sun. There was a bell beside the gate, which Dorothy rang. The big gate swung slowly open, and they all walked into a high arched room, its walls glistening with emeralds.

Before them stood a little man about the size of the Munchkins. He wore all green, and even his skin was of a greenish tint. At his side was a large green box.

The man asked, "What do you wish in the Emerald City?"

"We came here to see the Great Oz," said Dorothy.

The man was very surprised at this answer. "Few have seen Oz," he said. But I am the Guardian of the Gates, and I will take you to his palace. First you must put on these green glasses so that the brightness and glory of the Emerald City won't blind you. Even those who live in the city must wear spectacles night and day."

He opened the big box. It was filled with spectacles of every size and shape. The Guardian of the Gates found a pair that fit each of the travelers, and put the spectacles over their eyes.

Then the Guardian of the Gates put on his own glasses and told them he was ready to show them to the palace. Taking a big golden key from a peg on the wall, he opened another gate, and they all followed him into the streets of the Emerald City.

Even with their eyes protected by the green spectacles, Dorothy and her friends were at first dazzled by the brilliance of the wonderful city. The streets were lined with houses built of green marble and sparkling emeralds. The pavement was the same green marble, and where the blocks joined together, rows of emeralds glittered in the sun. The window panes were of green glass; even the sky above the city had a green tint, and the rays of the sun were green.

There were many people walking about, all dressed in green clothes, and with greenish skin. They looked at Dorothy and her strangely assorted company with wondering eyes, and the children all ran away and hid behind their mothers when they saw the Lion; but no one spoke to them. Many shops stood in the street, and Dorothy saw that everything in them was green.

There seemed to be no horses, nor animals of any kind; the men carried things around in little green carts, which they pushed before them. Everyone seemed happy and contented and prosperous.

The travelers came to the palace in the middle of the city. There was a soldier before the door, dressed in a green uniform and with a long green beard.

"Here are strangers," the Guardian of the Gates said to him, "and they demand to see the Great Oz."

"Step inside," answered the soldier, "and I will carry your message to him."

They passed through the palace gates and were led into a lovely green room.

The soldier left to relay his message. They had to wait a long time before the soldier returned. At last, he came back, and said: "Oz will see you, but each one of you must enter his presence alone, and he will admit but one each day. Therefore, I will have you shown to rooms in the palace where you may rest in comfort."

The next morning a green maiden came to fetch Dorothy, and she dressed Dorothy in one of the prettiest gowns, made of green brocaded satin. Dorothy put on a green silk apron and tied a green ribbon around Toto's neck, and they started for the throne room of the Great Oz.

Dorothy entered the throne room. It was a big, round room with a high arched roof, and everything was covered with large emeralds. In the center of the roof was a great light which made the emeralds sparkle.

A big throne of green marble, shaped like a chair and sparkling with gems, stood in the middle of the room. In the center of the chair was an enormous bald head, without a body to support it.

As Dorothy gazed upon the head in wonder and fear, the eyes turned slowly and looked at her sharply and steadily. Then the mouth moved, and Dorothy heard a voice say:

"I am Oz, the Great and Terrible. Who are you, and why do you seek me?"

Dorothy took courage and answered:

"I am Dorothy, the Small and Meek. I have come to you for help."

The eyes looked at her thoughtfully for a full minute. Then the voice asked:

"Where did you get the Silver Shoes?"

"I got them from the Wicked Witch of the East, when my house fell on her and killed her," she replied.

Oz asked, "What do you wish me to do?"

"Send me back to Kansas, where my Aunt Em and Uncle Henry are," she answered earnestly. "I am sure Aunt Em will be dreadfully worried over my being away so long."

"Well," said the Head, "You must do something for me in return. You must kill the Wicked Witch of the West."

"But I cannot!" exclaimed Dorothy, greatly surprised.

"You killed the Witch of the East and you wear the Silver Shoes, which bear a powerful charm. There is now but one Wicked Witch left in all this land, and when you can tell me she is dead I will send you back to Kansas—but not before."

Sorrowfully Dorothy left the throne room and went back to where her friends were waiting to hear what Oz had said to her. "There is no hope for me," she said sadly, "for Oz will not send me home until I have killed the Wicked Witch of the West; and that I can never do."

Her friends were sorry, but could do nothing to help her; so Dorothy went to her room and cried herself to sleep.

The next day, the Scarecrow was called to see Oz. Oz appeared to him as a lovely lady with silky wings.

The following day, the Tin Woodman went to see Oz. Oz appeared as a great monster to him. When the Lion went to see Oz, he was a great ball of fire. Each one of the travelers was asked to kill the Wicked Witch of the West. "What shall we do now?" asked Dorothy sadly.

"There is only one thing we can do," returned the Lion, "and that is to go to the land of the Winkies, seek out the Wicked Witch, and destroy her."

Therefore, it was decided to start upon their journey the next morning.

The soldier with the green whiskers led them through the streets of the Emerald City until they reached the room where the Guardian of the Gates lived. This officer unlocked their specta-cles to put them back in his great box, and then he politely opened the gate.

"Which road leads to the Wicked Witch of the West?" asked Dorothy.

"There is no road," answered the Guardian of the Gates. "No one ever wishes to go that way."

"How, then, are we to find her?" inquired the girl.

"That will be easy," replied the man, "for when she knows you are in the country of the Winkies, she will find you, and make you all her slaves. Take care;

for she is wicked and fierce, and may not allow you to destroy her. Keep to the West, where the sun sets, and you cannot fail to find her."

The Emerald City was soon left far behind. As they advanced, the ground became hillier and untilled.

In the afternoon the sun shone hot in their faces, for there were no trees to offer them shade; so that before night Dorothy and Toto and the Lion were tired, and lay down upon the grass and fell asleep, with the Woodman and the Scarecrow keeping watch.

The Wicked Witch of the West saw Dorothy and her friends a long distance off from her castle. She was so angry to find them in her country that she blew upon a silver whistle that hung around her neck.

At once there came running to her a great pack of wolves. They had long legs and fierce eyes and sharp teeth.

"Go to those people," said the Witch, "and tear them to pieces."

"Very well," said the wolf leader, and he dashed away at full speed, followed by the others.

It was lucky that the Scarecrow and the Woodman were wide awake and heard the wolves coming.

The Woodman seized his axe and chopped each wolf's head from its body as it came at him. When the Wicked Witch saw all her wolves lying dead, and the strangers still traveling through her country, she became angrier than before. She blew her silver whistle twice.

A great flock of crows came flying toward her. The Wicked Witch said to the

King Crow, "Fly at once to the strangers; peck out their eyes and tear them to pieces."

The crows flew toward Dorothy and her companions. The Scarecrow stood up and stretched out his arms, while his companions lay on the ground. When the crows saw him they were frightened, as these birds always are by scarecrows, and did not dare to come any nearer. But the King Crow said:

"It is only a stuffed man. I will peck his eyes out."

The King Crow flew at the Scarecrow, who caught it by the head and twisted its neck until it died. The Scarecrow killed all the crows this way.

When the Wicked Witch looked out again and saw that all her crows were dead, she got into a terrible rage. She called a dozen of her slaves, who were the Winkies, and gave them sharp spears, telling them to go to the strangers and destroy them.

The Winkies marched away until they came near to Dorothy. Then the Lion gave a great roar and sprang towards them, and the poor Winkies were so frightened that they ran back as fast as they could.

The Wicked Witch was furious. She put on her Golden Cap, which had a magic charm to it. Whoever owned it could call three times, and only three times, upon the Winged Monkeys, who would obey any order they were given. This was the last time the Wicked Witch could command the Winged Monkeys. There was a rushing of many wings and soon the Wicked Witch was surrounded by a crowd of Winged Monkeys.

The Witch commanded: "Go to the strangers who are within my land and

destroy them all, except the Lion," said the Wicked Witch. "Bring him to me, for I will harness him like a horse, and make him work."

The Winged Monkeys flew away to the place where Dorothy and her friends were walking. Some of the Monkeys seized the Tin Woodman and carried him over a country thickly covered with sharp rocks. They dropped the poor Woodman, who fell a great distance to the rocks, where he lay battered and dented.

Other Monkeys caught the Scarecrow and pulled all of the straw out of his clothes and head. The remaining Monkeys tied up the Lion with rope, then lifted him up and flew away with him to the Witch's castle, where he was placed in a small yard with a high iron fence around it, so that he could not escape.

But Dorothy they dared not harm, for the mark of the Good Witch's kiss was upon her forehead. The Winged Monkeys carried Dorothy to the castle, where they set her down upon the front doorstep. Then the leader of the Monkeys said to the Witch:

"We have obeyed you as far as we were able. The Tin Woodman and the Scarecrow are destroyed, and the Lion is tied up in your yard. The little girl we dare not harm, nor the dog she carries in her arms."

Then all the Winged Monkeys, with much chattering and noise, flew out of sight.

The Wicked Witch was both surprised and worried when she saw the mark on Dorothy's forehead and her charmed Silver Shoes, for she dared not hurt the girl in any way. But the Witch saw that Dorothy did not know the power the

Silver Shoes gave her. She thought, "I can still make her my slave, for she does not know how to use her power."

Then the Witch said to Dorothy, harshly and severely:

"Come with me; and see that you mind everything I tell you, for if you do not I will make an end of you, as I did of the Tin Woodman and the Scarecrow."

The Witch put her to work in the kitchen. Dorothy made up her mind to work as hard as she could, for she was glad the Wicked Witch had decided not to kill her. The Lion was kept in the courtyard and not fed until he would obey.

Every night, while the Witch was asleep, Dorothy carried the Lion food from the cupboard. After he had eaten, he would lie down on his bed of straw, and Dorothy would lie beside him and put her head on his soft, shaggy mane, while they talked of their troubles and tried to plan some way to escape. But they could find no way to get out of the castle, for it was constantly guarded by the Winkies, who were the slaves of the Wicked Witch and too afraid of her not to do as she told them.

The Wicked Witch longed to have the Silver Shoes, which the girl always wore, for they were very powerful. To get the Silver Shoes, the Wicked Witch played a trick on Dorothy. She placed a bar of iron in the middle of the kitchen floor, and then using magic, made the iron invisible to human eyes. When Dorothy walked across the floor she stumbled over the bar, not being able to see it, and fell down. She was not much hurt, but in her fall one of the Silver Shoes came off, and before she could reach it, the Witch had snatched it away and put it on her own foot.

Dorothy, seeing that she had lost one of her pretty shoes, grew angry. She picked up a bucket of water and dashed it over the Witch.

Instantly the Wicked Witch gave a loud cry of fear, and then, as Dorothy looked at her in wonder, the Witch melted away.

Dorothy picked out the Silver Shoe, which was all that was left of the old woman, cleaned and dried it with a cloth, and put it on her foot again. Then she ran out to the courtyard, where she set the Lion free and told him that the Wicked Witch of the West was dead. They went into the castle, where Dorothy called all the Winkies together and told them that they were no longer slaves.

There was great rejoicing among the yellow Winkies, for they had been made to work hard for many years for the Wicked Witch.

The Winkies thanked Dorothy by finding and fixing the Tin Woodman and the Scarecrow, who had been hurt by the Winged Monkeys. There was much rejoicing as all the travelers were reunited.

The next day the travelers bade the Winkies good-bye, for they were going back to the Emerald City to have Oz grant their wishes. The Winkies had grown so fond of the Tin Woodman that they begged him to come back and rule over them and the Yellow Land of the West.

Using the Witch's Golden Cap, Dorothy called the Winged Monkeys to carry them to Oz. In the Emerald City, they were admitted at once to see Oz. Each one of them expected to see the Wizard in the shape he had taken before, and all were greatly surprised when they saw no one in the room. The room was very still.

Presently they heard a solemn Voice, that seemed to come from somewhere near the top of the great dome, say:

"I am Oz, the Great and Terrible. Why do you seek me?"

"We have come to claim our promise, O Oz. Dorothy has killed the Wicked Witch," said the Tin Woodman.

"Is the Wicked Witch really destroyed?" asked the Voice.

"Yes," Dorothy answered, "I melted her with a bucket of water."

"Well, come to me tomorrow," said Oz.

"We shan't wait a day longer," replied the Scarecrow.

"You must keep your promises to us!" exclaimed Dorothy.

The Lion gave a loud roar, which made Toto jump away from him in alarm and tip over the screen that stood in a corner. Standing where the screen had been was a little old man, with a bald head and a wrinkled face, who seemed to be as much surprised as they were. The Tin Woodman asked, "Who are you?"

"I am Oz, the Great and Terrible," said the little man, in a trembling voice. "Please don't hurt me."

"I thought Oz was a great Head," said Dorothy.

"And I thought Oz was a lovely Lady," said the Scarecrow.

"And I thought Oz was a terrible Beast," said the Tin Woodman.

"And I thought Oz was a Ball of Fire," exclaimed the Lion.

"Are you not a Great Wizard?"

"No, I have been making believe. I am just a common man. Please don't tell or I shall be punished," he said.

"What about my brains?" asked the Scarecrow.

"Or my heart?" asked the Woodman.

"Or my courage?" asked the Lion.

"How shall I ever get home?" asked Dorothy.

"If you come back tomorrow, I shall help you all," said Oz. "I have played the Wizard so long that one more day won't matter."

The next morning the Scarecrow went to see Oz. Oz filled the Scarecrow's head with pins and needles, to make him "sharp". He cut a hole in the Woodman's chest and placed in it a small silk heart. To the Lion he gave a potion he called "courage." Then he turned to Dorothy.

"In order to get home," he said, "you must sew a big balloon out of silk. We will fill it with hot air to make it rise. It will carry us home over the desert."

"Us?" asked Dorothy. "Are you going with me?"

"Yes," said Oz. "I am from Omaha myself. I came here in a balloon a long time ago."

"I shall be glad to have your company," said Dorothy.

"Thank you," he answered. "Now, if you will help me sew the silk together, we will make our balloon."

When the balloon was made, Oz sent word to his people that he was going to visit a great brother Wizard who lived in the clouds. The news spread rapidly throughout the city and everyone came to see the wonderful sight.

Oz got into the balloon's basket and said to the people:

"I am now going away to make a visit. While I am gone the Scarecrow will rule over you. I command you to obey him as you would me."

The balloon was tugging hard at the rope that held it to the ground, for the air within it was hot, making the balloon rise.

"Come, Dorothy!" cried the Wizard. "Hurry up, or the balloon will fly away."

"I can't find Toto anywhere," replied Dorothy. Toto had run into the crowd to bark at a kitten, and Dorothy at last found him. She picked him up and ran towards the balloon.

She was within a few steps of it, and Oz was holding out his hands to help her into the basket, when, crack! went the ropes, and the balloon rose into the air without her.

"Come back!" she screamed. "I want to go, too!"

"I can't come back, my dear," called Oz from the basket. "Good-bye!"

"Good-bye!" everyone shouted.

Dorothy wept bitterly at the passing of her hope to get home to Kansas again; but when she thought it all over she was glad she had not gone up in a balloon. She also felt sorry at losing Oz, and so did her companions.

The Scarecrow was now the ruler of the Emerald City. The morning after the balloon had gone up with Oz, the four travelers met in the throne room and talked matters over.

The Scarecrow sat in the big throne and the others stood respectfully before him.

The Scarecrow was thinking, and his head bulged out so horribly that Dorothy feared it would burst.

"Let us call in the soldier with the green whiskers," he said, "and ask his

advice on how to get Dorothy home."

So the soldier was summoned and entered the throne room.

"Is there anyone who can help me get home?" asked Dorothy.

"Glinda, the Good Witch of the South, might. She is the most powerful of all the Witches."

"How can I get to her castle?" asked Dorothy.

"The road is to the South," he answered, "but it is full of danger."

The soldier then left them and the Scarecrow said:

"It seems that the best thing Dorothy can do is to travel to the Land of the South and ask Glinda to help her. If Dorothy stays here she will never get back to Kansas."

They all agreed to start out for Glinda's castle the next morning.

The first day's journey was through the green fields and bright flowers that surrounded the Emerald City. Soon they came to a thick wood. The Scarecrow tried to walk under a tree with wide-spreading branches, but was flung back. This did not hurt the Scarecrow, but it surprised him. He walked up to another tree, but its branches immediately seized him and tossed him back again.

The Woodman walked up to a tree and, when it tried to seize him, he cut it in two.

"Come on!" he shouted to the others. "Be quick!" They all ran forward and passed under the tree. The other trees of the forest did nothing to keep them back.

At the far edge of the wood they reached a wall made of china, which they made a ladder for and climbed over.

Before them was a great stretch of country with a floor as smooth and shining and white as the bottom of a big platter. Scattered around were many small houses and barns made of china, painted in the brightest colors. There were cows and sheep and horses and pigs and chickens, all made of china.

The people were milkmaids, shepherdesses, shepherds, princesses, and princes all made of china, even their clothes. They were so small that the tallest of them was no higher than Dorothy's knee. A jolly little clown with many cracks walked toward them, and Dorothy could see that in spite of his pretty clothes of red and yellow and green he had been mended in many places. The china people broke easily, so the travelers walked carefully through the country.

After climbing over another china wall, the travelers soon came to a gloomy forest. The Lion thought it was a wonderful forest, and that he would like to live there.

Before they had gone far they heard a low rumble, as of the growling of many wild animals. They came to an opening in the wood, in which were gathered hundreds of tigers and elephants and bears and wolves and foxes. The Lion explained that the animals were holding a meeting, and he judged by their snarling and growling that they were in great trouble.

As he spoke several of the beasts caught sight of him, and at once the great assemblage hushed as if by magic. The biggest of the tigers came up to the Lion and bowed, saying:

"Welcome, O King of Beasts! You have come in good time to fight our enemy and bring peace to all the animals of the forest once more."

"What is your trouble?" asked the Lion quietly.

"We are all threatened," answered the tiger, "by a tremendous monster, like a great spider, which has lately come into this forest. Not one of us is safe while this fierce creature is alive. We had called a meeting to decide how to take care of ourselves when you came among us."

"Where is this great spider now?" asked the Lion.

"There, among the oak trees," said the tiger.

The lion went to find the great spider. It was lying asleep when the Lion found him. He pounced upon the spider and knocked off his head, which had been placed upon a slender neck.

The Lion went back to where the beasts of the forest were waiting for him and said proudly:

"You need fear your enemy no longer."

Then the beasts bowed down to the Lion as their King, and he promised to come back and rule over them as soon as Dorothy was safely on her way to Kansas.

The four travelers came upon a steep hill, covered with great pieces of rock. They had just started forward when a voice said, "Keep back! This hill belongs to us, and no one may cross it." The man speaking stepped out from behind a rock. He was very short, with a big flat-topped head and a thick neck full of wrinkles. The man had no arms. The Scarecrow was not afraid of him, and started forward.

As quick as lightning the man's neck shot forward and his flat-topped head struck the Scarecrow, sending him tumbling down the hill. Almost as quickly as it came forward the head went back to the body, and the man laughed harshly as he said, "It isn't as easy as you think!"

Laughter came from the other rocks, and Dorothy saw hundreds of the armless Hammer-Heads upon the hillside, one behind every rock. She saw that there was no way around the Hammer-Heads, so she called the Winged Monkeys to carry the travelers to Glinda's castle.

Standing before the gates of the castle were three girls, dressed in red uniforms trimmed with gold braid. They inquired as to who the travelers were, then with Glinda's permission, led them into the castle.

They followed the soldier girls into a big room where Glinda sat upon a throne of rubies.

She was both beautiful and young to their eyes. Her hair was a rich red in color and fell in flowing ringlets over her shoulders. Her dress was pure white, and her eyes were blue.

"What can I do for you, my child?" she asked kindly.

Dorothy told the Witch of her adventures, and replied:

"My greatest wish now is to get back to Kansas."

"I am sure I can tell you of a way to get back to Kansas," Glinda said. "But first you must give me the Golden Cap."

Dorothy then gave Glinda the Golden Cap, and the Witch asked the

Scarecrow, the Tin Woodman, and the Lion: "What will you do when Dorothy has left us?"

"I will return to the Emerald City as its ruler," the Scarecrow replied.

"I will rule the Winkies," said the Tin Woodman.

"And I will rule the forest," said the Lion.

"My first command to the Winged Monkeys," said Glinda, "shall be to carry you all to your homes. Your Silver Shoes will carry you over the desert," Glinda told Dorothy, "Just click them together three times and say where you wish to go."

"I think I should like to go back to Kansas right away," said Dorothy.

Dorothy hugged and kissed her friends and Glinda goodbye, thanking Glinda for all the kindness she had shown to her friends and herself. It was a sad parting.

Dorothy held Toto in her arms, and having said one last good-bye she clapped the heels of her shoes together three times, saying:

"Take me home to Aunt Em!"

Instantly she was whirling through the air so swiftly that all she could see or feel was the wind whistling past her ears.

The Silver Shoes took but three steps, and then stopped so suddenly that Dorothy rolled over upon the grass several times before she knew where she was.

"Good gracious!" Dorothy cried, looking about her.

She was sitting on the broad Kansas prairie, and before her was the new farmhouse Uncle Henry built after the cyclone had carried away the old one. Uncle Henry was milking the cows in the barnyard, and Toto had jumped out of her arms and was running toward the barn, barking furiously.

Dorothy stood up and found she was in her stocking-feet. The Silver Shoes had fallen off in her flight through the air, and were lost forever in the desert.

Aunt Em had just come out of the house when she saw Dorothy running toward her.

"My darling child!" she cried, hugging Dorothy and covering her face with kisses. "Where in the world did you come from?"

"From the Land of Oz," said Dorothy. "And here is Toto, too. And oh, Aunt Em! I'm so glad to be at home again!"

THE END

THE ADVENTURES OF

PINOCCHIO

by Carlo Collodi

Illustrated by Greg Hildebrandt

THE ADVENTURES OF
PINOCCHIO

There once was a piece of wood lying in the carpenter shop of Master Antonio. Master Antonio decided to make a table leg out of the wood, but to his surprise, when he struck it, the wood cried out.

Just then his friend Geppetto, a little old man with a yellow wig, came in. Whenever anyone wanted to make Geppetto angry they would just comment on his yellow wig, calling him *Polendina*, which means "yellow corn pudding".

Geppetto told Master Antonio:

"I want to make a beautiful wooden marionette. With it I intend to go around the world to earn my living. What do you think?"

"Bravo, Polendina!" cried a tiny voice which came from no one knew where.

On hearing himself called Polendina, Master Geppetto turned red and facing the carpenter, said to him angrily: "Why do you insult me?"

"Who is insulting you?"

"You called me Polendina."

"I did not."

"Yes."

"No."

"Yes."

"No."

And growing angrier each moment, they began to fight.

When the fight was over, Master Antonio and Geppetto agreed to be friends.

"Well then, Master Geppetto," said the carpenter, "what is it you want?"

"I want a piece of wood to make a marionette. Will you give it to me?" asked Geppetto.

Master Antonio, very glad indeed, gave Geppetto the piece of wood which had cried out. Geppetto thanked Master Antonio, and limped away toward home.

Geppetto lived in a one-room house that was neat and comfortable. The furniture was very simple: an old chair, a rickety bed, and a tumble-down table. A fireplace full of burning logs was painted on the wall opposite the door. Over the fire was painted a pot full of something, which kept boiling happily away and sending up clouds of what looked like real steam.

As soon as he reached home, Geppetto took his tools and began to cut and shape the wood into a marionette.

"What shall I call him?" he said to himself. "I think I'll call him Pinocchio. That is a lucky name."

After choosing the name for his marionette, Geppetto set to work on the hair, forehead, and eyes. Fancy his surprise when he noticed that these eyes moved and then stared at him. Geppetto, seeing this, said:

"Ugly wooden eyes, why do you stare so?"

There was no answer.

After the eyes, Geppetto made the nose, which began to stretch as soon as it was finished. It stretched until it became so long it seemed endless. Poor Geppetto kept cutting it, but the more he cut, the longer the nose grew. In despair he let it alone.

Next he made the mouth. No sooner was it finished than it began to laugh and poke fun at him.

"Stop laughing!" Geppetto yelled angrily.

The mouth stopped laughing, but it stuck out a long tongue.

Not wishing to start an argument, Geppetto made believe he saw nothing and went on with his work. After the mouth, he made the chin, then the neck, the shoulders, the stomach, the arms, and the hands.

As he was about to put the last touches on the fingertips, Geppetto felt his wig being pulled off. His yellow wig was in the marionette's hand. "Pinocchio, give me my wig!" he cried.

But instead of giving it back, Pinocchio put it on his own head.

Geppetto became very sad and cried out:

"Pinocchio, you wicked boy! You are not yet finished and you start out by being impudent to your poor old father. Very bad, my son, very bad!"

And he wiped away a tear.

The legs and feet still had to be made. As soon as they were done, Geppetto felt a sharp kick on the tip of his nose.

"I deserve it!" he said to himself. "I should have thought of this before I made him. Now it's too late!"

He took hold of the marionette under the arms and put him on the floor to teach him to walk.

Pinocchio's legs were so stiff that he could not move them, but Geppetto held his hand and showed him how to put out one foot after the other.

When his legs were limbered up, Pinocchio started walking by himself, and ran all around the room. He came to the open door, and with one leap he was out onto the street. Away he flew!

Poor Geppetto ran after him but was unable to keep up.

"Catch him! Catch him!" Geppetto kept shouting. But the people in the street, seeing a wooden marionette running like the wind, stood still to stare and laugh.

At last, by sheer luck, a policeman happened along, grabbed Pinocchio by the nose, and returned him to Master Geppetto.

Geppetto seized Pinocchio by the back of the neck to take him home. As he was doing so, he shook Pinocchio two or three times and said to him angrily:

"We're going home now. When we get home, then we'll settle this matter!"

Pinocchio, on hearing this, threw himself on the ground and refused to take another step. Many people gathered around.

"Poor marionette," called out a man. "I am not surprised he doesn't want to go home. Geppetto, no doubt, will beat him unmercifully, he is so mean and cruel!"

"Geppetto looks like a good man," added another, "but with boys he's a real tyrant. If we leave that poor marionette in his hands he may tear him to pieces!"

They said so much that, finally, the policeman ended matters by setting Pinocchio at liberty and dragging Geppetto to prison.

Pinocchio ran home. Upon reaching home, he slipped into the room, locked the door, and threw himself on the floor, happy at his escape.

But his happiness lasted only a short time, for just then he heard someone saying:

"Cri-cri-cri!"

"Who is calling me?" asked Pinocchio, greatly frightened.

"I am!"

Pinocchio turned and saw a large cricket crawling slowly up the wall.

"Tell me, cricket, who are you?"

"I am the Talking Cricket and I have been living in this room for more than one hundred years."

"Today, however, this room is mine," said the marionette, "and if you wish to do me a favor, get out now, and don't turn around even once."

"I refuse to leave this spot," answered the cricket, "until I have told you a great truth."

"Tell it, then, and hurry."

"Woe to boys who refuse to obey their parents and run away from home! They will never be happy in this world, and when they are older they will be very sorry for it."

"Sing on cricket, as you please. What I know is that tomorrow, at dawn, I leave this place forever. If I stay here the same thing will happen to me which happens to all other boys and girls. They are sent to school to study. Let me tell you, I hate to study! It's much more fun, I think, to chase after butterflies, climb trees, and steal birds' nests."

"Poor little silly! Don't you know that if you go on like that, you will grow into a perfect donkey and that you'll be the laughingstock of everyone?"

"Keep still, you ugly cricket!" cried Pinocchio.

But the cricket continued:

"If you do not like going to school, why don't you at least learn a trade, so that you can earn an honest living?"

"Shall I tell you something?" asked Pinocchio, who was beginning to lose patience. "Of all the trades in the world, there is only one that really suits me: that of eating, drinking, sleeping, playing, and wandering around from morning till night."

"Those who follow that trade always end up in the hospital or in prison," said the cricket. I feel sorry for you, because you are a marionette and, what is much worse, you have a wooden head."

At these last words, Pinocchio jumped up in a fury, took a hammer from the bench, and threw it with all his strength at the Talking Cricket.

Perhaps he did not think he would strike it, but he hit the cricket straight on its head.

With a last weak "cri-cri-cri" the poor cricket fell from the wall, dead!

If the cricket's death scared Pinocchio at all, it was only for a very few moments. For, as night came on, Pinocchio grew hungry, and realized he had eaten nothing as of yet.

Pinocchio's hunger grew until he was as ravenous as a bear. He searched about the room. Finding nothing, he decided to go out for a walk in the near-by village, in the hope of finding some charitable person who might give him a bit of bread.

But the village was dark and deserted, and he returned home tired, wet, and hungry.

As he no longer had any strength left with which to stand, he sat down on a little stool and put his two feet on the stove to dry them.

There he fell asleep, and while he slept, his wooden feet began to burn. Slowly, they blackened and turned to ashes.

Pinocchio snored away happily as if his feet were not his own. At dawn he opened his eyes just as a loud knocking sounded at the door.

"Who is it?" he called, yawning and rubbing his eyes.

"It is I," answered Geppetto.

The poor marionette, who was still half-asleep, had not yet found out that his two feet were burned off. As soon as he heard his father's voice, he jumped up from his seat to open the door, but, as he did so, he staggered and fell headlong to the floor.

"Open the door for me!" Geppetto shouted from the street.

"Father, dear Father, I can't," answered Pinocchio in despair, crying and rolling on the floor. "Someone has eaten my feet."

Geppetto, thinking that all these tears and cries were only pranks, climbed up the side of the house and went in through the window.

At first he was very angry, but on seeing Pinocchio stretched out on the floor without feet, he felt very sad and sorrowful. Picking him up from the floor, he cried:

"My little Pinocchio, my dear little Pinocchio! How did you burn your feet?"

Pinocchio told Geppetto of his adventures, and that he was still very hungry.

Geppetto gave Pinocchio three pears, which were supposed to be for his breakfast.

Pinocchio would not eat the pears unless they were peeled. Geppetto peeled the pears and gave them back to Pinocchio, who devoured them, then began to grumble that he wanted a new pair of feet. He promised not to run away from home again, to study, and to be a good boy.

Master Geppetto made two new feet for Pinocchio. As soon as the marionette felt his new feet, he jumped with joy.

"To show you how grateful I am to you, Father, I'll go to school now. But to go to school I need a suit of clothes."

Geppetto did not have a penny in his pocket, so he made his son a little suit of paper, a pair of shoes from the bark of a tree, and a tiny cap from a bit of dough.

"In order to go to school, I need an A-B-C book," said Pinocchio.

Geppetto then sold his only coat to buy the book for his son.

Pinocchio, unable to restrain his tears, jumped on his father's neck and kissed him over and over.

Pinocchio hurried to school, thinking of the fantastic things he would learn. As he walked, there came the sound of pipes and drums in the distance.

He stopped to listen. The sounds came from a small village along the shore. Pinocchio said to himself:

"Today I'll follow the pipes, and tomorrow I'll go to school. There's always plenty of time to go to school."

He ran toward the sounds, and the pipe and drum grew louder.

Suddenly he found himself in a large square, full of people standing in front of a little wooden building painted in brilliant colors. It was a Marionette Theater. It cost four pennies to get in.

Pinocchio, who was curious to know what was going on inside, sold his schoolbook to a ragpicker nearby for the price of a ticket.

Pinocchio ran into the Marionette Theater. The curtain was up and the performance had started. Harlequin and Pulcinella were reciting on the stage and, as usual, they were threatening each other with sticks and blows.

The theater was full of people, enjoying the spectacle and laughing at the antics of the two marionettes.

The play continued for a few minutes, and then suddenly Harlequin stopped talking. Turning toward the audience, he pointed to the rear of the orchestra, yelling wildly at the same time:

"Look, look! Am I asleep or awake? Do I really see Pinocchio there?"

"Yes, yes! It is Pinocchio!" screamed Pulcinella.

"It is! It is!" shrieked Signora Rosaura, peeking in from the side of the stage.

"It is Pinocchio!" yelled all the marionettes, pouring out of the wings. "It is our brother Pinocchio! Hurrah for Pinocchio!"

"Pinocchio, come up to me!" shouted Harlequin. "Come to the arms of your wooden brothers!"

Pinocchio leaped onto the stage.

The marionettes greeted him with shrieks of joy, warm embraces, knocks, and friendly greetings.

The audience, seeing that the play had stopped, became angry and began to yell:

"The play, the play, we want the play!"

The yelling was of no use, for the marionettes just made more noise and, lifting up Pinocchio on their shoulders, carried him around the stage in triumph.

At that very moment, the director came out of his room. He had a fearful appearance: a long black beard, a mouth as wide as an oven, teeth like yellow fangs, and two eyes like glowing red coals. In his huge, hairy hands was a long whip.

Everyone was scared at the unexpected apparition.

"Why have you brought such excitement into my theater?" the huge fellow angrily asked Pinocchio.

"Believe me, your Honor, the fault was not mine."

"Enough! Be quiet! I'll take care of you later."

As soon as the play was over, the director went to the kitchen, where a fine big lamb was cooking. He needed more wood, so he told Harlequin and Pulcinella to bring Pinocchio to him, to use as firewood.

Harlequin and Pulcinella hesitated, but they were afraid of their master and followed his orders. They returned carrying poor Pinocchio, who was wriggling and squirming and crying pitifully:

"Father, save me! I don't want to die! I don't want to die!"

When Fire Eater (this was really his name) saw the poor marionette being brought in to him, struggling with fear and crying, he felt sorry for him and began to sneeze. Fire Eater, instead of crying, sneezed when he felt sad.

Fire Eater then set Pinocchio free. He gave Pinocchio five gold pieces to bring home to his poor old father, Geppetto.

Pinocchio, beside himself with joy, set out toward home.

He had gone barely half a mile when he met a lame fox and a blind cat. The lame fox leaned on the cat, and the blind cat let the fox lead him along.

"Good morning, Pinocchio," said the fox, greeting him courteously.

"How do you know my name?" asked the marionette.

"I know your father well."

"Where have you seen him?"

"I saw him yesterday standing at the door of his house."

"And what was he doing?"

"He was in his shirt sleeves trembling with cold."

"Poor Father! But, after today, God willing, he will suffer no longer."

"Why?"

"Because I have become a rich man."

"You, a rich man?" said the fox, and he began to laugh out loud. The cat was laughing also, but tried to hide it by stroking his long whiskers.

"There is nothing to laugh at," cried Pinocchio angrily. "I am very sorry to make your mouth water, but these, as you know, are five new gold pieces."

And he pulled out the gold pieces which Fire Eater had given him.

At the cheerful tinkle of the gold, the fox unconsciously held out his paw that was supposed to be lame, and the cat opened wide his two eyes till they looked like live coals, but he closed them again so quickly that Pinocchio did not notice.

"And may I ask," inquired the fox, "what you are going to do with all that money?"

"First of all," answered the marionette, "I want to buy a fine new coat for my father, and after that, I'll buy an A–B–C book for myself."

Suddenly, the fox stopped in his tracks and, turning to the marionette, said to him:

"Do you want to double your gold pieces?"

"Yes, but how?" asked Pinocchio.

"Instead of returning home, come with us to the City of Simple Simons. There you can bury your money in a field and overnight your gold pieces will grow into a tree, which is loaded with gold pieces."

Pinocchio agreed to go with the fox and the cat, to grow a tree with many more gold pieces than he already had.

Cat and fox and Pinocchio walked until evening. At last, dead tired, they came to the Inn of the Red Lobster.

"Let us stop here a while," said the fox, "to eat a bite and rest. At midnight we'll start out again, for at dawn tomorrow we must be at the Field of Wonders."

They went into the Inn and sat down to supper.

When supper was done the fox said to the Innkeeper: "Give us two good rooms, one for Mr. Pinocchio and the other for me and my friend. Remember to call us at midnight sharp, for we must continue on our journey."

"Yes, sir," answered the Innkeeper, winking at the fox and the cat.

As soon as Pinocchio was in bed, he slept and dreamed of a tree of gold coins.

In the middle of his dream, Pinocchio was awakened by three loud knocks at the door. The Innkeeper had come to tell him that midnight had struck.

"Are my friends ready?" the marionette asked him.

"Indeed, yes! They went two hours ago. The cat received a telegram which said that his first-born was sick. He could not even wait to say good-bye to you."

"Did they pay for the supper?"

"How could they do that? They did not want to offend by not allowing you the honor of paying. They said to meet them at the Field of Wonders, at sunrise."

Pinocchio paid a gold piece for the three suppers and started on his way.

As he walked, Pinocchio noticed a tiny insect glowing on the trunk of a tree.

"Who are you?" he asked.

"I am the Ghost of the Talking Cricket," answered the little being in a faint voice that sounded as if it came from a far-away world. "I want to give you a few words of good advice. Return home and give the four gold pieces you have left to your poor old father who is weeping because he has not seen you for many a day."

"Tomorrow he will be rich. These four gold pieces will become two thousand."

"Don't listen to those who promise you wealth overnight, my boy. As a rule they are either fools or swindlers! Listen to me and go home."

"But I want to go on!"

"Boys who insist on having their own way sooner or later come to grief."

There was silence for a minute and the light of the Talking Cricket disappeared as if someone had snuffed it out. Once again the road was plunged into darkness.

Pinocchio continued walking until he heard a slight rustle among the leaves.

Two figures, wrapped in black sacks, leaped toward him as if they were ghosts.

"Here they come!" Pinocchio said to himself, and, not knowing where to hide the gold pieces, he stuck all four of them under his tongue.

He tried to run away, but hardly had he taken a step, when he felt his arms grasped and heard two horrible, deep voices say to him: "Your money or your life!"

On account of the gold pieces in his mouth, Pinocchio could not say a word, so he tried with head and hands and body to show, as best he could, that he was only a poor marionette without a penny in his pocket.

"Come, come, less nonsense, and out with your money!" cried the two thieves.

Once more, Pinocchio's head and hands said, "I haven't a penny."

"Out with that money or you're a dead man," said the taller of the two assassins. And after having killed you, we will kill your father also."

"No, no, not my Father!" cried Pinocchio, wild with terror; but as he screamed, the gold pieces tinkled together in his mouth.

"You rascal! You have the money hidden under your tongue. Out with it!"

One of them grabbed the marionette by the nose and the other by the chin, and they pulled him unmercifully from side to side in order to make him open his mouth.

But the marionette's lips might as well have been nailed together. They would not open.

In desperation the smaller of the two assassins pulled out a long knife from his pocket, and tried to pry Pinocchio's mouth open with it.

Quick as a flash, the marionette sank his teeth deep into the assassin's hand, bit it off and spat it out. He was surprised to see it was not a hand, but a cat's paw.

Pinocchio freed himself from the claws of his assailers and, leaping over the bushes along the road, ran swiftly across the fields. His pursuers were after him at once.

After running many miles, Pinocchio was exhausted. He was afraid he would have to surrender to his pursuers. Suddenly he saw a little cottage gleaming white among the trees of the forest.

Pinocchio reached the door of the cottage and knocked. No one answered.

He knocked again, harder than before, for behind him he heard the steps and the labored breathing of his persecutors. The same silence followed.

In despair, Pinocchio began to kick and bang against the door. At the noise, a window opened and a lovely maiden looked out. She had azure hair and a face white as wax. Her eyes were closed and her hands crossed on her breast. With a voice so weak that it hardly could be heard, she whispered:

"Go away. No one here can help you."

After these words, the little girl disappeared and the window closed without a sound.

"Oh, Lovely Maiden with Azure Hair," cried Pinocchio, "open, I beg of you. Take pity on a poor boy who is being chased by two assass—"

He did not finish, for two powerful hands grasped him by the neck and the same two horrible voices growled threateningly: "Now we have you! We will hang you until you drop the coins."

Pinocchio trembled. The two assassins hung the marionette on a tree and waited for Pinocchio to die. Little by little, Pinocchio's eyes closed. As he was about to die, he thought of his poor old father, and said:

"Oh, Father, dear Father! If you were only here!"

Luckily, the lovely maiden with azure hair once again looked out of her window. Filled with pity at the sight of poor Pinocchio, she clapped her hands sharply together three times. A falcon appeared, who flew to Pinocchio and brought him to the fairy (for the lovely maiden with azure hair was none other than a very kind fairy who had lived, for more than a thousand years, in the vicinity of the forest).

The fairy put Pinocchio to bed and called for Crow, Owl, and Talking Cricket, who were the best doctors in the neighborhood. The crow pronounced the marionette dead, but the owl said that he was alive.

The cricket said: "I say that a wise doctor, when he does not know what he is talking about, should know enough to keep his mouth shut. However, I know this marionette. He is a vagabond and a runaway."

Pinocchio, who until then had been very quiet, shuddered so hard that the bed shook.

"The marionette is a disobedient son who is breaking his father's heart!"

Pinocchio hid his face under the sheets and sobbed.

"When the dead weep, they are beginning to recover," said the crow solemnly.

"I disagree," said the owl, "I think that when the dead weep, it means they do not want to die."

As soon as the three doctors had left the room, the fairy touched Pinocchio on the forehead, and noticed that he was burning with fever.

She handed Pinocchio medicine, saying lovingly to him:

"Drink this, and in a few days you'll be up and well."

Pinocchio did not want to drink the medicine because it was bitter, but the fairy said that if he did not drink it he would die. So Pinocchio drank the liquid. In a twinkling, he felt fine. With one leap he was out of bed and into his clothes.

The fairy, seeing him run and jump around the room gay as a bird on wing, said to him:

"My medicine was good for you, after all, wasn't it?"

"Good indeed! It has given me new life."

"Come here now and tell me how it came about that you found yourself in the hands of the assassins."

Pinocchio told the fairy his story, and that he had lost his gold pieces. That was a lie, for he had them in his pocket.

As he spoke, his nose grew longer. The more he lied, the more it grew.

The fairy sat looking at him and laughing.

"Why do you laugh?" the marionette asked her, worried now at the sight of his growing nose.

"I am laughing at your lies."

"How do you know I am lying?"

"Lies, my boy, are known in a moment. There are two kinds of lies, lies with short legs and lies with long noses. Yours, just now, happen to have long noses."

Pinocchio, not knowing where to hide his shame, tried to escape from the room, but his nose had become so long that he could not get it out of the door.

The fairy felt sorry for him and called for a thousand woodpeckers to peck away his nose, so that it was the same size as before.

"How good you are, my fairy," said Pinocchio, "and how much I love you!"

"I love you, too," answered the fairy, "and if you wish to stay with me, you may be my little brother and I'll be your good little sister."

"I should like to stay—but what about my poor father?"

"Your father has been sent for and before night he will be here."

"Really?" cried Pinocchio joyfully. "Then, my good fairy, if you are willing, I should like to go to meet him. I cannot wait to kiss that dear old man, who has suffered so much for my sake."

"Surely; go ahead, but be careful not to lose your way. Take the wood path and you'll surely meet him."

Pinocchio set out, and soon ran into the fox and cat. He foolishly agreed to continue on with them to the Field of Wonders.

They walked and walked for half a day and at last came to the town called the City of Simple Simons. It was filled with mangy animals.

Through this crowd of poor animals, a beautiful coach passed now and again. Within it sat either a fox, a hawk, or a vulture.

Pinocchio, fox, and cat passed through the city and, just outside the walls, they stepped into a field, which looked like any other field. Pinocchio buried his gold pieces and went away for twenty minutes as the fox told him to, so that his tree could grow.

Upon returning, Pinocchio saw that there was no tree, and that his coins had been dug up. The fox and cat had robbed him.

In desperation, he ran to the city and went straight to the courthouse to report the robbery to the magistrate. The judge was a large gorilla, venerable with age. A flowing white beard covered his chest and he wore gold-rimmed spectacles from which the glasses had dropped out.

Pinocchio told the judge his pitiful tale. When the marionette had no more to say, the judge rang a bell.

At the sound, two large dogs appeared, dressed in policemens' uniforms.

Then the magistrate, pointing to Pinocchio, said in a very solemn voice:

"This poor simpleton has been robbed of four gold pieces. Take him, therefore, and throw him into prison."

The marionette, on hearing this sentence passed upon him, was thoroughly stunned. He tried to protest, but the two officers clapped their paws on his mouth and hustled him away to jail.

There he had to remain for four months. When he was released, Pinocchio ran away from the city, to find the house of the lovely fairy. He was determined to see his father

and his fairy, and to become a good boy.

Pinocchio finally came to the spot where the fairy's house had once stood. It was no longer there. In its place lay a small marble slab, which bore this sad inscription:

Here lies the lovely fairy with azure hair
who died of grief when abandoned
by her little brother Pinocchio

The poor marionette was heartbroken at reading these words, and burst into bitter tears. He cried all night, until a pigeon flew by in the morning and carried him to the seashore, where his father, Geppetto, had been looking for him. Geppetto had been searching for his son for a long time.

Upon arriving at the seashore, Pinocchio spotted a little boat tossing amongst the wild waves of the rough sea. It was his father, Geppetto! Pinocchio stood on a high rock and waved and cried out to his father.

It looked as if Geppetto, though far away from the shore, recognized his son, for he took off his cap and waved also. Suddenly a huge wave came and the boat disappeared.

Pinocchio jumped into the sea and cried out:

"I'll save him! I'll save my father!"

The marionette, being made of wood, floated easily along and swam like a fish in the rough water. In a twinkling, he was far away from land.

Pinocchio, spurred on by the hope of finding his father and of being in time to save him, swam all night long. In the morning he saw an island and, tired and soaked, stopped to rest.

The marionette took off his clothes and laid them on the sand to dry. He looked over the waters for his father. He searched and searched, but saw nothing except sea and sky.

A dolphin, swimming by, told Pinocchio that his father had probably been swallowed up by the huge shark that had recently been invading the waters. He also told Pinocchio how to get to the nearest village, where he could get some food.

This said, Pinocchio headed toward the village.

In the village, everyone was busy working.

A little woman went by carrying two water jugs.

"Good woman, will you allow me to have a drink from one of your jugs?" asked Pinocchio, who was burning up with thirst.

"With pleasure, my boy!" she answered, setting the two jugs on the ground before him.

When Pinocchio had had his fill, he grumbled, as he wiped his mouth:

"My thirst is gone. If I could only as easily get rid of my hunger!"

On hearing these words, the good little woman immediately said:

"If you help me to carry these jugs home, I'll give you a slice of bread, some cauliflower with white sauce, cake and jam."

Pinocchio said: "Very well. I'll take the jug home for you."

The jug was very heavy, and the marionette, not being strong enough to carry it with his hands, had to put it on his head.

When they arrived home, the little woman made Pinocchio sit down at a small table and placed before him the bread, the cauliflower, and the cake. Pinocchio devoured it. His stomach seemed a bottomless pit.

His hunger finally appeased, he raised his head to thank his kind benefactress. But he had not looked at her long when he gave a cry of surprise. The woman was his little fairy!

"You rascal of a marionette! How did you know it was I?" she asked, laughing.

"My love for you told me who you were."

"Do you remember? You left me when I was a little girl and now you find me a grown woman. I am so old, I could almost be your mother!"

"I am very glad of that, for then I can call you mother instead of sister. For a long time I have wanted a mother, just like other boys. But how did you grow so quickly?"

"That's a secret!"

"Tell it to me. I also want to grow a little."

"But you can't grow," answered the fairy. "Marionettes never grow. They are born marionettes, they live as marionettes, and they die as marionettes."

"Oh, I'm tired of always being a marionette!" cried Pinocchio disgustedly. "It's about time for me to grow into a man as everyone else does."

"And you will if you deserve it—"

"Really? What can I do to deserve it?"

"If you are good, if you go to school and study and do not tell lies, you can become a real boy," answered the fairy.

"I promise. I want to become a good boy and be a comfort to my father. Where is my poor father now?"

"I do not know."

"Will I ever be lucky enough to find him and embrace him once more?"

"I think so. Indeed, I am sure of it."

At this answer, Pinocchio's happiness was very great. He grasped the fairy's hands and kissed them hard.

The fairy had forgiven Pinocchio for running away. She said: "From now on, I'll be your own little mother.

"Oh! How lovely!" cried Pinocchio, jumping with joy.

"Beginning tomorrow," said the fairy, "you'll go to school every day."

Pinocchio finally agreed, for he wanted to be a real boy.

In the morning, bright and early, Pinocchio went to school.

The boys in the classroom laughed and played tricks on him. But they did not play

tricks for long, for Pinocchio gave one of the boys a sound kick with his wooden foot, and a jab with his elbow, which made the boys favor Pinocchio after that.

As the days passed into weeks, even the teacher praised him, for he saw him attentive, hard working, and wide awake, always the first to come in the morning, and the last to leave when school was over.

Pinocchio's only fault was that he had too many friends who were well-known rascals, who cared not a bit for study or for success.

The teacher warned him each day, and even the good fairy repeated to him many times:

"Take care, Pinocchio! Those bad companions will sooner or later make you lose your love for study. Some day they will lead you astray."

"There's no such danger," answered the marionette, shrugging his shoulders and pointing to his forehead as if to say, "I'm too wise."

So it happened that one day, as he was walking to school, he met some boys who ran up to him and said:

"Have you heard the news?"

"No!"

"A shark as big as a mountain has been seen near the shore."

"Really? I wonder if it could be the same one I heard of when my father was drowned?"

"We are going to see it. Are you coming?"

"No, not I. I must go to school."

"What do you care about school? You can go there tomorrow."

"Do you know what I'll do?" said Pinocchio. "For certain reasons of mine, I, too, want to see that shark; but I'll go after school. I can see him then as well as now."

"Poor simpleton!" cried one of the boys. "Do you think that a fish of that size will stand there waiting for you? He turns and off he goes, and no one will ever be the wiser."

"How long does it take from here to the shore?" asked Pinocchio.

"One hour there and back."

"Very well, then. Let's see who gets there first!" cried Pinocchio.

At the signal, the little troop, with books under their arms, dashed across the fields. Pinocchio led the way, running as if on wings, the others following as fast as they could.

Going like the wind, Pinocchio took but a very short time to reach the shore. He glanced all about him, but there was no sign of a shark. The sea was as smooth as glass.

The boys had played a trick on him.

"What now?" he said angrily to them. "What's the joke?"

"Oh, the joke's on you!" cried his tormentors, laughing more heartily than ever, and dancing gayly around the marionette.

"And that is—?"

"That we have made you stay out of school to come with us. Aren't you ashamed of being such a goody-goody, and of studying so hard? You never have a bit of enjoyment."

The boys went on tormenting Pinocchio, and they eventually started to fight with him. They threw books at him. One book hit another boy, named Eugene, in the head. Eugene, pale as a ghost, cried out faintly:

"Oh, Mother, help! I'm dying!" and fell senseless to the ground.

All the boys except Pinocchio were scared and ran away. Pinocchio called to him, saying: "Eugene! My poor Eugene! Open your eyes and look at me! Why don't you answer?"

Pinocchio went on crying and moaning. Again and again he called to his little friend, when suddenly he heard heavy steps approaching.

He looked up and saw two tall policemen near him. Thinking Pinocchio had hurt the boy with his schoolbook, they told Pinocchio:

"Get up as quickly as you can and come along with us."

"But I am innocent."

"Come with us!"

Before starting out, the officers called out to several fishermen passing by in a boat and said to them:

"Take care of this little fellow who has been hurt. Take him home and bind his wounds. Tomorrow we'll come for him."

They then took hold of Pinocchio and, putting him between them, said to him in a rough voice:

"March! And go quickly, or it will be the worse for you!"

They did not have to repeat their words. The marionette walked swiftly along the road to the village, but he suffered at the thought of passing under the windows of his good little fairy's house. What would she say on seeing him between two policemen?

They had just reached the village, when a sudden gust of wind blew off Pinocchio's cap and made it go sailing far down the street.

"Would you allow me," the marionette asked the policemen, "to run after my cap?"

"Very well, go; but hurry."

The marionette went, picked up his cap—but instead of putting it on his head, he stuck it between his teeth and raced toward the sea.

The policemen, judging that it would be very difficult to catch him, sent a large dog after him, one that had won first prize in all the dog races. Pinocchio ran fast and the dog ran faster.

The dog, named Alidoro, had almost caught Pinocchio, when the marionette made a great leap into the sea.

Alidoro tried to stop, but as he was running very fast, he couldn't, and he, too, landed far out in the sea. The dog could not swim. He beat the water with his paws to hold himself up, but the harder he tried, the deeper he sank. As he stuck his head out once more, the poor fellow's eyes were bulging and he barked out wildly, "I drown! Help, Pinocchio! Save me from death!"

At those cries of suffering, the marionette, who after all had a very kind heart, was moved to compassion. He turned toward the poor animal and said to him:

"But if I help you, will you promise not to bother me again by running after me?"

"I promise! Only hurry, for if you wait another second, I'll be dead and gone!"

Pinocchio caught hold of Alidoro's tail and dragged him to shore.

The poor dog was so weak he could not stand. He had swallowed so much salt water that he was swollen like a balloon. However, Pinocchio, not wishing to trust him too much, threw himself once again into the sea. As he swam away, he called out:

"Good-bye, Alidoro, good luck and remember me to your family!"

"Good-bye, little Pinocchio," answered the dog. "A thousand thanks for having saved me from death. You did me a good turn, and, in this world, what is given is always returned. If the chance comes, I shall be there."

Pinocchio went on swimming close to shore. At last he thought he had reached a safe place. Glancing up and down the beach, he saw the opening of a cave out of which rose a spiral of smoke.

Suddenly he felt something under him lifting him up higher and higher. Pinocchio was in a huge net, amid a crowd of fish of all kinds and sizes, who were fighting and struggling desperately to free themselves.

At the same time, he saw a fisherman come out of the cave, a fisherman so ugly that Pinocchio thought he was a sea monster. In place of hair, his head was covered by a thick bush of green grass. His skin was green, his eyes were green, and his long beard was green.

When the fisherman pulled the net out of the sea, he cried out joyfully:

"Blessed Providence! Once more I'll have a fine meal of fish!"

The fisherman took the net and the fish into the dark cave. In the middle of it, a pan

full of oil sizzled over a smoky fire. The fisherman covered the fish in flour, and began to place them in the sizzling pan.

The last to come out of the net was Pinocchio.

As soon as the fisherman pulled him out, his green eyes opened wide with surprise, and he cried out in fear:

"What kind of fish is this? I don't remember ever eating anything like it."

"I am a marionette," said Pinocchio, "I am not a fish."

The fisherman decided to eat Pinocchio anyway. He rolled him in flour and got ready to put Pinocchio in the frying pan. Pinocchio trembled with fright.

Just then a large dog, attracted by the odor of the boiling oil, came running into the cave.

"Get out!" cried the fisherman threateningly, still holding onto the marionette, who was covered with flour.

But the poor dog was very hungry, and whining and wagging his tail, he tried to say:

"Give me a bite of the fish and I'll go in peace."

"Get out, I say!" repeated the fisherman.

And he drew back his foot to give the dog a kick.

Then the dog, who, being really hungry, would take no refusal, turned in a rage toward the fisherman and bared his terrible fangs. And at that moment, a pitiful little voice was heard saying: "Save me, Alidoro; if you don't, I fry!"

The dog immediately recognized Pinocchio's voice. Great was his surprise to find that the voice came from the little flour-covered bundle that the fisherman held in his hand.

With one great leap, Alidero grasped that bundle in his mouth and, holding it tightly between his teeth, ran through the door and disappeared.

The fisherman, angry at seeing his meal snatched from under his nose, ran after the dog, but a bad fit of coughing made him stop and turn back.

Meanwhile, Alidoro, as soon as he had found the road which led to the village, stopped and dropped Pinocchio softly to the ground.

"How much I do thank you!" said the marionette.

"It is not necessary," answered the dog. "You saved me once, and what is given is always returned. We are in this world to help one another."

They bid each other farewell as good friends.

Pinocchio, left alone, walked toward a little hut near by, where an old man sat at the door sunning himself, and asked:

"Tell me, good man, have you heard anything of a poor boy with a wounded head, whose name was Eugene?"

"The boy was brought to this hut. He is alive and has already returned home."

Pinocchio was overjoyed at hearing this news. He set out at once to return to the fairy's house. Upon reaching the house, Pinocchio was so tired that he fell asleep on t he doorstep.

When he awoke, Pinocchio found himself stretched out on a sofa and the fairy was seated near him.

"This time also I forgive you," said the fairy to him. "But be careful not to get into mischief again."

Pinocchio promised to study and to behave himself. And he kept his word for the remainder of the year. At the end of it, he passed first in all his examinations, and his report was so good that the fairy said to him happily:

"Tomorrow your wish will come true."

"And what is it?"

"Tomorrow you will cease to be a marionette and will become a real boy."

Pinocchio was beside himself with joy. All his friends and schoolmates must be invited to celebrate the great event. He went to give out invitations.

When Pinocchio went to look for Lamp-Wick, the laziest boy in school, he could not find him.

Finally he discovered Lamp-Wick hiding near a farmer's wagon.

"What are you doing there?" asked Pinocchio, running up to him.

"I am waiting for midnight to strike to go far-away to the Land of Toys. A place where there is no school and you play all day long. Why don't you come, too?"

"I? Oh, no! But I will wait here to see you go."

Finally the wagon arrived, packed with boys.

It was drawn by twenty-four donkeys, all wearing shoes made of leather, just like the ones boys wear.

The driver of the wagon was a jolly fat man, with a small and wheedling voice.

No sooner had the wagon stopped than the little fat man turned to Lamp-Wick. With bows and smiles, he asked:

"Tell me, my fine boy, do you also want to come to my wonderful country?"

"Indeed I do."

"Hope on the top of the coach then."

To Pinocchio he said:

"What about you, my love?"

Pinocchio hesitated, but with much prodding from Lamp-Wick, finally agreed to go. There were no seats left, so Pinocchio had to ride one of the donkeys. The donkey did not like it at first, but the man finally made the donkey allow Pinocchio to ride it.

While the donkeys galloped along the stony road, the marionette thought he heard a very quiet voice whispering to him:

"Poor silly! You have done as you wished. But you are going to be a sorry boy before very long. A day will come when you will weep bitterly, even as I am weeping now— but it will be too late!"

At these whispered words, Pinocchio grew more and more frightened. He jumped to the ground, ran up to the donkey on whose back he had been riding, and taking his nose in his hands, looked at him. He saw that the donkey was weeping—just like a boy!

"Hey, Mr. Driver!" cried the marionette. "Do you know what strange thing is happening here! This donkey weeps."

"Let him weep. Ignore it and ride along."

Pinocchio obeyed, and toward dawn the wagon finally reached the Land of Toys.

The population of this land was composed wholly of boys. The oldest were about fourteen years of age, the youngest, eight. In the street was a racket from boys shouting and blowing trumpets. Everywhere boys were playing games, such as marbles, tag, ball, and circus. Generals in full uniform led regiments of cardboard soldiers. Everywhere there was great pandemonium and laughter.

The squares were filled with small wooden theaters, overflowing with boys from morning till night, and on the walls of the houses were the words:

Hurrah for the Land of Toys!

Down with arithmetic! No more school!

As soon as they had set foot in that land, Pinocchio, Lamp-Wick, and all the other boys who had traveled with them started out on a tour of investigation. They wandered everywhere, and became everybody's friend.

What with entertainments and parties, the hours, the days, the weeks passed like lightning.

Five months passed and the boys continued playing and enjoying themselves from morning till night, without ever going to school.

One morning, after five months had past, Pinocchio awoke to find that his ears had grown at least ten full inches, into donkey's ears!

He began to cry and scream, but the more he shrieked, the longer and the more hairy his ears grew. Pinocchio put a bag over his head, and went out to find his friend Lamp-Wick. He thought that Lamp-Wick was to blame for bringing him to the Land of Toys in the first place.

With his head covered he went out. He looked everywhere for Lamp-Wick, but he was not to be found. He asked everyone whom he met about him, but no one had seen him. In desperation, Pinocchio returned home and knocked at the door.

"Who is it?" asked Lamp-Wick from within.

"It is I!" answered the marionette.

"Wait a minute."

After a full half hour the door opened. There in the room stood Lamp-Wick, with a bag over his head.

At the sight of that bag, Pinocchio realized that Lamp-Wick was, indeed, turning into a donkey as well. They threw off their bags and, instead of feeling sorry for each other, the friends made fun of one another.

They laughed and laughed, and laughed again—laughed till they ached—laughed till they cried.

But all of a sudden Lamp-Wick stopped laughing. He tottered and almost fell. Pale as a ghost, he turned to Pinocchio and said:

"Help, Pinocchio! I can no longer stand up."

"I can't either," cried Pinocchio; and his laughter turned to tears as he stumbled about helplessly.

They had hardly finished speaking, when both of them fell on all fours and began running and jumping around the room. As they ran, their arms turned into legs, their faces lengthened into snouts, their backs became covered with long gray hairs, and they grew tails.

Instead of moans and cries, they burst forth into loud donkey brays, which sounded very much like, "Haw! Haw! Haw!"

At that moment, a loud knocking was heard at the door and a voice called to them:

"Open! I am the driver of the wagon which brought you here. Open, I say, or beware!"

Very sad and downcast were the two poor little fellows as they stood and looked at each other. Outside the room, the driver grew more and more impatient, and finally gave the door such a violent kick that it flew open. With his usual sweet smile on his lips, he looked at Pinocchio and Lamp-Wick and said to them:

"Fine work, boys! You have brayed well, so well that I recognized your voices immediately, and here I am."

The man brought them to market to sell. Pinocchio was sold to the owner of a circus, who wanted to teach him to do tricks for his audiences.

Pinocchio knew that if he had gone to school and studied hard, he never would have become a circus donkey.

After putting him in a stable, his new master filled his manger with straw, which Pinocchio did not like at first but finally ate because he was very hungry.

His new owner was very mean, and often whipped Pinocchio. He taught Pinocchio to jump and bow, to dance a waltz and a polka, and to stand on his head.

It took poor Pinocchio three long months and cost him many lashings before he was pronounced perfect.

The day came at last when Pinocchio's master was able to announce an extraordinary performance. The announcements, posted all around the town, and written in large letters, read thus:

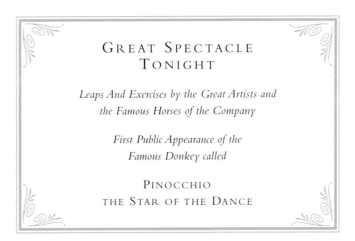

That night the theater was filled with boys and girls of all ages and sizes, impatiently

waiting to see the famous donkey dance.

The manager of the circus appeared, in a black coat, white knee breeches, and patent

leather boots, to announce Pinocchio's dance. Pinocchio then appeared in the circus ring,

handsomely adorned, to do tricks for the audience. Near the end of his act, he fell down

and became lame, barely able to limp back to his stable.

The next morning the veterinarian declared that Pinocchio would be lame for the

rest of his life.

"What do I want with a lame donkey?" said the manager to the stableboy. "Take him

to the market and sell him."

A buyer was soon found who wanted to use Pinocchio's skin to make a drumhead.

As soon as the buyer had paid for the donkey, he took Pinocchio to a high cliff over-

looking the sea, put a stone around his neck, tied a rope to one of his hind feet, and

threw him into the water.

Pinocchio sank immediately. His new master sat on the cliff waiting for him to

drown, so as to skin him and make himself a drumhead.

After fifty minutes of waiting, the man thought his donkey was drowned, and pulled

the rope, which he had tied to Pinocchio's leg. The man pulled and pulled, until at last he saw something appear on the surface of the water. But instead of a dead donkey, a very much alive marionette, wriggling and squirming like an eel.

The man could not believe what he saw. What had happened to his donkey?

The fairy had been protecting Pinocchio from drowning, and sent a thousand fish to bite away the part of him that was a donkey. Upon rising to the surface, Pinocchio bid the man farewell and swam off into the sea.

Far off in the sea, Pinocchio suddenly saw a horrible sea monster stick its head out of the water. It had an enormous head with a huge mouth, wide open, showing three rows of gleaming teeth.

Pinocchio tried to swim away, but the sea monster, who was in fact the shark, swallowed him.

When he recovered his senses the marionette could not remember where he was. Around him all was darkness. He listened for a few moments and heard nothing. Once in a while a cold wind blew on his face. At first he could not understand where that wind was coming from, but after a while he understood that it came from the lungs of the monster. The shark was suffering from asthma, so that whenever he breathed a storm seemed to blow.

Pinocchio thought he saw a faint light in the distance. He walked toward the light. The closer he got, the brighter and clearer grew the tiny light. On and on he walked till finally he found a little table set for dinner and lighted by a candle stuck in a glass bottle; near the table sat a little old man, white as the snow, eating live fish.

At this sight, the poor marionette was filled with such great and sudden happiness that he almost dropped in a faint. He wanted to laugh, he wanted to cry, he wanted to say a thousand and one things, but all he could do was to stand still, stuttering and stammering brokenly. At last, with a great effort, he was able to let out a scream of joy and, opening wide his arms he threw them around the old man's neck.

"Oh, Father, dear Father! Have I found you at last? Now I shall never, never leave you again!"

"Are my eyes really telling me the truth?" answered the old man, rubbing his eyes. "Are you really my own dear Pinocchio?"

"Yes, yes, yes! It is I! Look at me! And you have forgiven me, haven't you? Oh, my dear Father, how good you are! And to think that I—oh, but if you only knew how many misfortunes have fallen on my head and how many troubles I have had!"

Pinocchio told his father of his troubles, and Geppetto told Pinocchio of how his boat had been swallowed by the shark.

"There is no time to lose," Pinocchio said, "We must try to escape."

"Escape! How?"

"We can run out of the shark's mouth and dive into the sea. Follow me."

Pinocchio took the candle in his hand, to light the way, and started off on the long walk through the stomach and the whole body of the shark. When they reached the throat of the monster, they stopped for a while to wait for the right moment in which to make their escape.

The shark, being very old and suffering from asthma and heart trouble, was obliged to sleep with his mouth open. Because of this, Pinocchio was able to catch a glimpse of the sky filled with stars, as he looked up through the shark's open jaws.

"The time has come for us to escape," he whispered, turning to his father. "The shark is fast asleep. The sea is calm and the night is as bright as day. Follow me closely, dear Father, and we shall soon be saved."

No sooner said than done. They climbed up the throat of the monster till they came to that immense open mouth. There they had to walk on tiptoes, for if they tickled the shark's long tongue he might awaken. They jumped over three rows of teeth. Before they took the last great leap, the marionette said to his father:

"Climb on my back and hold on tightly to my neck. I'll take care of everything else."

As soon as Geppetto was comfortably seated on his shoulders, Pinocchio dived into the water and started to swim. The shark continued to sleep so soundly that not even a cannon shot would have awakened him.

Pinocchio swam as hard as he could, trying to find shore. After quite a while he began to feel discouraged, and his strength was leaving him. He felt he could not go on much longer, and the shore was still far away.

He swam a few more strokes. Then he turned to Geppetto and cried out weakly:

"Help me, Father! Help, for I am dying!"

Father and son were about to drown when a tunny came up out of the sea, to give them a ride to shore. The tunny had been in the stomach of the shark as well, and followed Pinocchio's example to escape.

Geppetto and Pinocchio climbed on the tunny's back and soon they were on the shore.

In the meantime day had dawned.

Pinocchio offered his arm to Geppetto, who was so weak he could hardly stand, and said to him:

"Lean on my arm, dear father, and let us go find a house or hut, where they will be kind enough to give us a bite of bread and a bit of straw to sleep on. We will walk very slowly, and if we feel tired we can rest by the wayside."

They had not taken a hundred steps when they came upon fox and cat. After pretending to be lame for so many years, the fox had really become lame. The cat, after pretending to be blind for so many years, had really lost the sight of both eyes.

"Oh, Pinocchio," the fox cried in a tearful voice. "Give us some alms, we beg of you! We are old, tired, and sick."

"Sick!" repeated the cat.

"Addio, false friends!" answered the marionette. "You cheated me once, but you will

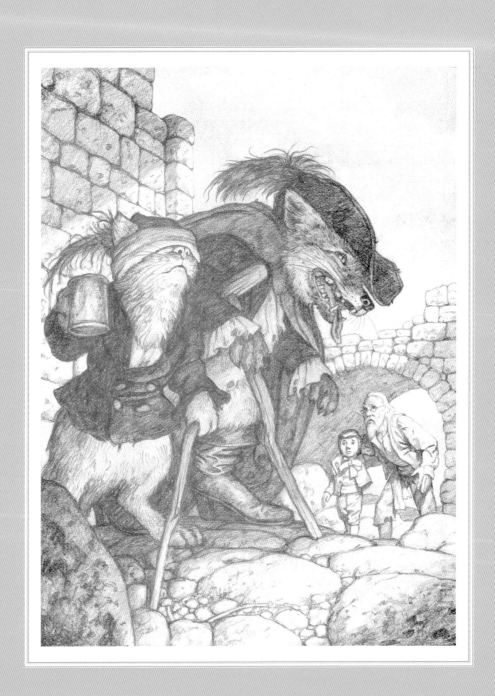

never catch me again. If you are poor; you deserve it! Remember the old proverb which says: `Stolen money never bears fruit.'"

Waving good-bye to them, Pinocchio and Geppetto calmly went on their way. After a few more steps, they saw a tiny cottage built of straw.

They went and knocked at the door.

"Who is it?" said a little voice from within.

"A poor father and a poorer son, without food and with no roof to cover them," answered the marionette.

"Turn the key and the door will open," said the same little voice.

Pinocchio turned the key and the door opened. As soon as they went in, they looked here and there and everywhere but saw no one.

"Oh—ho, where is the owner of the hut?" cried Pinocchio, very much surprised.

"Here I am, up here!"

Father and son looked up to the ceiling, and there on a beam sat the Talking Cricket. The Talking Cricket had forgiven Pinocchio for throwing a hammer at him, and offered a bed of straw to the father and son.

Pinocchio laid his father on it and said to the Talking Cricket:

"Tell me, little cricket, where shall I find a glass of milk for my poor father?"

"Three fields away from here lives Farmer John. He has some cows. Go there and he will give you what you want."

Pinocchio ran all the way to Farmer John's house. The farmer told Pinocchio that if he drew water for him, he would give the marionette a glass of milk.

"Until today," said the farmer, "my donkey has drawn the water for me, but now that poor animal is dying."

"Will you take me to see him?" said Pinocchio.

"Gladly."

Pinocchio spied the little donkey in the stable, and went to him. He asked the donkey: "Who are you?"

At this question, the donkey opened weary, dying eyes and answered: "I am Lamp-Wick."

Then he closed his eyes and died.

"Oh, my poor Lamp-Wick," said Pinocchio in a faint voice, as he wiped his eyes with some straw he had picked up from the ground.

From that day on, for more than five months, Pinocchio got up every morning to work to get a glass of warm milk for his poor old father, who grew stronger and better day by day. But he was not satisfied with this. He learned to make baskets of reeds and sold them. With the money he received, he and his father were able to keep from starving.

One morning Pinocchio saw the fairy's maid. The maid said that the fairy was very ill. Pinocchio gave the maid fifty pennies to give to his poor fairy. He worked harder than ever to help his poor father and his fairy.

In the evening the marionette studied by lamplight. Little by little his diligence was rewarded. He succeeded, not only in his studies, but also in his work, and a day came when he put enough money together to keep his old father comfortable and happy.

One night, as he slept, Pinocchio dreamt of his fairy, who kissed him and said: "Bravo, Pinocchio! Always try to do good, and you will be happy."

At that very moment, Pinocchio awoke. Upon looking himself over, he saw that he was no longer a marionette, but a real live boy! He looked all about him and instead of the usual walls of straw, he found himself in a beautifully furnished little room. Pinocchio ran into the other room, where Geppetto was working at his new bench.

Pinocchio joyfully said: "How ridiculous I was when I was a puppet! And how glad I am now that I have become a real boy!"

THE END

ALICE'S
ADVENTURES
IN WONDERLAND

by Lewis Carroll

ILLUSTRATED BY GREG HILDEBRANDT

ALICE'S ADVENTURES IN WONDERLAND

Alice was beginning to get very tired of sitting by her sister on the bank, and of having nothing to do. Once or twice she had peeped into the book her sister was reading, but it had no pictures or conversations in it, 'and what is the use of a book,' thought Alice 'without pictures or conversation?'

So she was considering in her own mind whether the pleasure of making a daisy chain would be worth the trouble of getting up and picking the daisies, when suddenly a White Rabbit with pink eyes ran close by her.

There was nothing so *very* remarkable in that; nor did Alice think it so very much out of the way to hear the Rabbit say to itself, "Oh dear! Oh dear! I shall be late!" But when the Rabbit actually took a watch out of its waistcoat-pocket, and looked at it, and then hurried on, Alice started to her feet, for it flashed across her mind that she had never before seen a rabbit with either a waistcoat-pocket, or a watch to take out of it, and burning with curiosity, she ran across the field after it and fortunately was just in time to see it pop down a large rabbit hole under the hedge.

In another moment down went Alice after it, never once considering how in the world she was to get out again.

The rabbit-hole went straight on like a tunnel for some ways, and then dipped suddenly down, so suddenly that Alice had not a moment to think about stopping herself before she found herself falling down a very deep well.

Either the well was very deep, or she fell very slowly, for she had plenty of time as she went down to look about her and to wonder what was going to happen next. First, she tried to look down and make out what she was coming to, but it was too dark to see anything. Then she looked at the sides of the well, and noticed that they were filled with cupboards and bookshelves; here and there she saw maps and pictures hung upon pegs.

Down, down, down. There was nothing else to do, so Alice soon began talking. "Dinah'll miss me very much tonight, I should think!" (Dinah was the cat.) "I hope they'll remember her saucer of milk at tea-time." And here Alice began to get rather sleepy. She felt that she was dozing off, and had just begun to dream when suddenly, down she came upon a heap of sticks and dry leaves, and the fall was over.

Alice was not a bit hurt, and she jumped to her feet in a moment. Before her was another long passage, and the White Rabbit was still in sight, hurrying down it. There was not a moment to be lost: away went Alice like the wind, and was just in time to hear it say, as it turned a corner, "Oh my ears and whiskers, how late it's getting!" She was close behind it when she turned the corner, but the Rabbit was no longer to be seen. She found herself in a long, low hall, which was lit by a row of lamps hanging from the roof.

There were doors all round the hall, but they were all locked; and when

Alice had tried every door, she walked sadly down the middle, wondering how she was ever to get out again.

Suddenly she came upon a little three-legged table made of solid glass; there was nothing on it except a tiny golden key, and Alice's first thought was that it might belong to one of the doors of the hall; but, alas! Either the locks were too large, or the key was too small, but at any rate it would not open any of them. However, on the second time round, she came upon a low curtain she had not noticed before, and behind it was a little door about fifteen inches high. She tried the little golden key in the lock, and to her great delight it fitted!

Alice opened the door and found that it led into a small passage. She knelt down and looked along the passage into the loveliest garden you ever saw. How she longed to get out of that dark hall, and wander about among those beds of bright flowers and those cool fountains, but she could not even get her head though the doorway. 'Oh, how I wish I could close up like a telescope!' thought Alice. 'I think I could, if I only knew how to begin.' For, you see, so many out-of-the-way things had happened lately that Alice had begun to think that very few things were really impossible.

There seemed to be no use in waiting by the little door, so she went back to the table. This time she found a little bottle on it, and round the neck of the bottle was a paper label with the words 'DRINK ME' beautifully printed on it in large letters.

It was all very well to say 'DRINK ME,' but wise little Alice was not going to do that in a hurry. "No, I'll look first," she said, "and see whether it's marked 'poison' or not." However, this bottle was not marked 'poison,' so Alice ventured to taste it, and finding it very nice, she very soon finished it off.

"What a curious feeling!" said Alice. "I must be closing up like a telescope."

And so it was indeed. She was now only ten inches high, and her face brightened up at the thought that she was now the right size for going through the little door into that lovely garden. Alas for poor Alice, when she got to the door, she found she had forgotten the little golden key, and when she went back to the table for it, she found she could not possibly reach it.

Soon her eye fell on a little glass box that was lying under the table. She opened it, and found in it a very small cake, on which the words 'EAT ME' were beautifully marked in currants. She ate a little bit, and she was quite surprised to find that she remained the same size: to be sure, this generally happens when one eats cake, but Alice had got so much into the way of expecting nothing but out-of-the-ordinary things to happen. So she set to work, and very soon finished off the cake.

"Curiouser and curiouser!" cried Alice. "Now I'm opening out like the largest telescope that ever was!" Just then her head struck against the roof of the hall: in fact she was now more than nine feet high, and she at once took up the little golden key and hurried off to the garden door.

Poor Alice! It was as much as she could do, lying down on one side, to look through into the garden with one eye; but to get through was more hopeless than ever and she began to cry.

After a time she heard a little pattering of feet in the distance. It was the White Rabbit returning. With a pair of white kid gloves in one hand and a large fan in the other, he came trotting along in a great hurry, uttering to himself as he came, "Oh! The Duchess! Oh! Won't she be savage if I've kept her

waiting!" Alice felt so desperate that she was ready to ask help of anyone, so, when the Rabbit came near her, she began, in a low, timid voice, "If you please, sir—" The Rabbit started violently, dropped the white kid gloves and the fan, and scurried away into the darkness as hard as he could go.

Alice took up the fan and gloves, and, as the hall was very hot, she kept fanning herself all the time she went on talking: "How strange everything is today!" As she said this she looked down at her hands, and was surprised to see that she had put on one of the Rabbit's little white gloves. 'How can I have done that?' she thought. 'I must be growing small again.' She went to the table to measure herself by it, and found that, as nearly as she could guess, she was now about two feet high, and was going on shrinking rapidly. She soon found out that the cause of this was the fan she was holding, and she dropped it hastily, just in time to avoid shrinking away altogether.

"That was a narrow escape!" said Alice, and she ran back to the little door: but, alas! The door was shut again, and the little golden key was lying on the glass table as before, 'and things are worse than ever,' thought the poor child, 'for I never was so small as this before, never!'

As she said these words her foot slipped, and in another moment, splash! She was up to her chin in salt water. Her first idea was that she had somehow fallen into the sea. However, she soon made out that she was in the pool of tears, which she had wept when she was nine feet high.

"I wish I hadn't cried so much!" said Alice, as she swam about, trying to find her way out.

Just then she heard something splashing about in the pool a little way off. At first she thought it must be a walrus or hippopotamus, but then she remembered how small she was now, and she soon made out that it was only a mouse that had slipped in like herself.

'Would it be of any use,' thought Alice, 'to speak to this mouse? Everything is so out-of-the-way down here, that I should think very likely it can talk.' So she began: "O Mouse, do you know the way out of this pool? I am very tired of swimming about here!" The Mouse looked at her rather inquisitively, and seemed to her to wink with one of its little eyes, but it said nothing.

'Perhaps it doesn't understand English,' thought Alice; 'I daresay it's a French mouse.' So she began again: "*Ou est ma chatte?*" which was the first sentence in her French lesson book. The Mouse gave a sudden leap out of the water, and seemed to quiver all over with fright. "Oh, I beg your pardon!" cried Alice hastily, afraid that she had hurt the poor animal's feelings. "I quite forgot you didn't like cats."

"Not like cats!" cried the Mouse, in a shrill, passionate voice. "Would you like cats if you were me?"

"Well, perhaps not," said Alice in a soothing tone. "Don't be angry about it. And yet I wish I could show you our cat Dinah: I think you'd take a fancy to cats if you could only see her. She is such a dear quiet thing," Alice went on, "and she sits purring so nicely by the fire—and she's such a capital one for catching mice—oh, I beg your pardon!" cried Alice. For the mouse was swimming away from her as hard as it could go, and making quite a commotion in the pool as it went.

So she called softly after it, "Mouse dear! Do come back again, and we won't talk about cats, if you don't like them!" When the Mouse heard this, it turned round and swam slowly back to her. Its face was quite pale and it said

in a low trembling voice, "Let us get to the shore, and then I'll tell you my history, and you'll understand why it is I hate cats."

It was high time to go, for the pool was getting quite crowded with the birds and animals that had fallen into it: there were a Duck and a Dodo, a Lory and an Eaglet, and several other curious creatures. Alice led the way, and the whole party swam to the shore.

They were indeed a strange-looking party that assembled on the bank— the birds with draggled feathers, the animals with their fur clinging close to them, and all dripping wet, cross, and uncomfortable.

The first question of course was, how to get dry again. They had a consultation about this, and after a few minutes it seemed quite natural to Alice to find herself talking with them, as if she had known them all her life.

At last the Mouse called out, "Sit down, all of you, and listen to me! I'll soon make you dry enough!" They all sat down at once, in a large ring, with the Mouse in the middle. Alice kept her eyes anxiously fixed on it, for she felt sure she would catch a bad cold if she did not get dry soon.

"Ahem!" said the Mouse with an important air, "are you all ready? This is the driest thing I know."

"'William the Conqueror, whose cause was favored by the pope, was soon submitted to by the English, who wanted leaders, and had been of late much accustomed to usurpation and conquest.'"

"How are you getting on now, my dear?" it continued, turning to Alice as it spoke.

"As wet as ever," said Alice in a melancholy tone. "It doesn't seem to dry me at all."

"In that case," said the Dodo solemnly, rising to its feet, "I move that the meeting adjourn for the immediate adoption of more energetic remedies."

"Speak English!" said the Eaglet. "I don't know the meaning of half those long words, and, what's more, I don't believe you do either!"

"What I was going to say," said the Dodo in an offended tone, "was, that the best thing to get us dry would be a Caucus-race."

"What is a Caucus-race?" asked Alice.

"The best way to explain it is to do it," said the Dodo. First it marked out a race course, in a sort of circle and then all the party were placed along the course, here and there. There was no 'One, two, three, and away,' but they began running when they liked, and left off when they liked, so that it was not easy to know when the race was over. However, when they had been running half an hour or so, and were quite dry again, the Dodo suddenly called out "The race is over!" and they all crowded round, panting, and asking, "Who has won?"

This question the Dodo could not answer without a great deal of thought, and it sat for a long time with one finger pressed upon its forehead while the rest waited in silence. At last the Dodo said, "*everybody* has won, and all must have prizes."

"But who is to give the prizes?" quite a chorus of voices asked.

"Why, she, of course," said the Dodo, pointing to Alice with one finger; and the whole party at once crowded around her, calling out in a confused way, "Prizes! Prizes!"

Alice had no idea what to do, and in despair she put her hand in her pocket, and pulled out a box of comfits and handed them round as prizes. There was exactly one a-piece all round.

"But she must have a prize herself, you know," said the Mouse.

"Of course," the Dodo replied very gravely. "What else have you got in your pocket?" he went on, turning to Alice.

"Only a thimble," said Alice sadly.

"Hand it over here," said the Dodo.

Then they all crowded around her once more, while the Dodo solemnly presented the thimble, saying "We beg your acceptance of this elegant thimble." When it had finished this short speech, they all cheered. Alice thought the whole thing very absurd, but she simply bowed, and took the thimble.

In a little while, Alice again heard a little pattering of footsteps in the distance. It was the White Rabbit, trotting slowly back again, and looking anxiously about as it went as if it had lost something, and she heard it muttering to itself, "The Duchess! Oh my fur and whiskers! She'll get me executed, as sure as ferrets are ferrets! Where can I have dropped them, I wonder?" Alice guessed that it was looking for the fan and the pair of gloves, and she began hunting for them, but they were nowhere to be seen—everything seemed to have changed since her swim in the pool, and the great hall, with the glass table and the little door, had vanished completely.

Very soon the Rabbit noticed Alice and called out to her, "Mary Ann, what are you doing out here? Run home this moment and fetch me a pair of gloves and a fan!" Alice ran off at once in the direction it pointed to, without trying to explain the mistake it had made. 'He took me for his housemaid,' she thought to herself as she ran.

Soon Alice came upon a neat little house, on the door of which was a bright brass plate with the name 'W. Rabbit' engraved upon it. She went in without knocking, and hurried upstairs.

She found her way to a tidy room with a table, and on it (as she had hoped) a fan and two or three pairs of tiny white gloves. She took up the fan and a pair of the gloves, and was just going to leave the room when her eye fell upon a little bottle that stood near the looking-glass. There was no label this time with the words 'DRINK ME' but nevertheless she uncorked it and put it to her lips. 'I know something interesting is sure to happen,' she said to herself, 'so I'll just see what this bottle does. I do hope it'll make me grow large again, for really I'm quite tired of being such a tiny little thing!'

It did so indeed, and much sooner than she had expected. Before she had drunk half the bottle, she found her head pressing against the ceiling, and had to stoop. She hastily put down the bottle, saying to herself, 'That's quite enough—I hope I shan't grow any more—as it is, I can't get out the door!'

Alas, she went on growing, and soon had to kneel on the floor. In another minute there was not even room for this, and she tried the effect of lying down with one elbow against the door, and the other arm curled round her head. Still she went on growing, and as a last resource, she put one arm out of the window, and one foot up the chimney, and said to herself, 'Now I can do no more. What will become of me?'

Luckily for Alice, the little magic bottle had now had its full effect, and she grew no larger. After a few minutes she heard a voice outside, and stopped to listen.

"Mary Ann! Mary Ann!" said the voice. "Fetch me my gloves this moment!" Then came a little pattering of feet on the stairs. Alice knew it was the Rabbit coming to look for her.

Presently, the Rabbit came up to the door and tried to open it; but, as the door opened inwards, and Alice's elbow was pressed hard against it, that attempt proved a failure. Alice heard it say to itself, "Then I'll go round and get in at the window."

'That you won't' thought Alice, and after waiting till she fancied she heard the Rabbit just under the window, she suddenly spread out her hand and made a snatch in the air. She did not get hold of anything, but she heard a little shriek and a fall, and a crash of broken glass.

Next came an angry voice—the Rabbit's—"Pat! Pat! Where are you?" And then a voice she had never heard before, "Sure then I'm here!"

"Now tell me, Pat, what's that in the window?"

"It's an arm, yer honour!"

"Well, it's got no business there. Go and take it away!"

There was a long silence after this and she waited for some time without hearing anything more. At last came a rumbling of little cartwheels, and the sound of a good many voices all talking together. She made out the words, "Bill! The master says you're to go down the chimney!"

'So Bill's got to come down the chimney, has he?' said Alice to herself. 'I wouldn't be in Bill's place. This fireplace is narrow, but I think I can kick a little!'

She drew her foot as far down the chimney as she could, and waited till she heard a little animal scratching and scrambling about in the chimney close above her. Then, she gave one sharp kick, and waited to see what would happen next.

The first thing she heard was a general chorus of, "There goes Bill!" Then the Rabbit's voice—"Catch him!" then silence, and then another confusion of voices—"What happened to you? Tell us all about it!"

At last came a little squeaking voice. "Well, I hardly know—all I know is, something comes at me like a Jack-in-the-box, and up I goes like a sky-rocket!"

"So you did, old fellow!" said the others.

"We must burn the house down!" said the Rabbit's voice, and Alice called out as loud as she could, "If you do. I'll set Dinah on you!"

There was a dead silence instantly. After a minute or two, Alice heard the Rabbit say, "A barrowful will do, to begin with."

"A barrowful of what?" thought Alice; but she had not long to doubt, for the next moment a shower of little pebbles came rattling in the window and some of them hit her in the face. 'I'll put a stop to this,' she said to herself, and shouted out, "You'd better not do that again!" which produced another dead silence.

Alice noticed with some surprise that the pebbles were all turning into little cakes as they lay on the floor, and a bright idea came into her head. 'If I eat one of these cakes,' she thought, 'it's sure to make some change in my size; and as it can't possibly make me larger, it must make me smaller.'

So she swallowed one of the cakes, and was delighted to find that she began shrinking. As soon as she was small enough, she ran out of the house and found a crowd of little animals and birds waiting outside. They all made a rush at Alice the moment she appeared; but she ran off as hard as she could and soon found herself safe in a thick wood.

'The first thing I've got to do,' said Alice to herself, 'is to grow to my right size again; and the second thing is to find my way into that lovely garden. I think that will be the best plan.'

While she was peering about anxiously among the trees, a sharp bark over her head made her look up in a great hurry.

An enormous puppy was looking down at her with large round eyes, stretching out one paw, trying to touch her. Alice tried hard to whistle to it, but she was terribly frightened that it might be hungry, in which case it would be very likely to eat her up.

Hardly knowing what she did, she picked up a little bit of stick and held it out to the puppy; the puppy jumped into the air off all its feet at once, and with a yelp of delight, rushed at the stick. Then the puppy began a series of short charges at the stick, till at last it sat down a good way off, with its tongue hanging out of its mouth and its great eyes half shut.

This seemed to Alice a good opportunity for making her escape, so she set off at once running until she was quite tired and out of breath, and till the puppy's bark sounded quite faint in the distance.

"What a dear little puppy it was!" said Alice, as she leant against a buttercup to rest herself. "I should have liked teaching it tricks—if I'd only been the right size to do it! Oh dear! I'd nearly forgotten that I've got to grow up again! I suppose I ought to eat or drink something or other, but the great question is, what?"

The great question certainly was, what? Alice looked all round her at the flowers and the blades of grass, but she did not see anything that looked like the right thing to eat or drink under the circumstances. There was a large mushroom growing near her, about the same height as herself. She stretched herself up on tiptoe, and peeped over the edge of it. Her eyes immediately met those of a large caterpillar that was sitting on the top with its arms folded, quietly smoking a long hookah, and taking not the smallest notice of her or of anything else.

The Caterpillar and Alice looked at each other for some time in silence: until at last the Caterpillar took the hookah out of its mouth and addressed her in a languid, sleepy voice.

"Who are you?" said the Caterpillar.

Alice replied, rather shyly, "I—I hardly know, sir, just at present—at least I know who I was when I got up this morning, but I think I must have been changed several times since then."

"What do you mean by that?" said the Caterpillar sternly. "Explain yourself!"

"I can't explain myself, I'm afraid, sir," said Alice, "because I'm not myself, you see."

"I don't see," said the Caterpillar.

"I'm afraid I can't put it more clearly," Alice replied very politely, "for I can't understand it myself; and being so many different sizes in a day is very confusing."

"It isn't," said the Caterpillar.

"Well, perhaps you haven't found it so yet," said Alice. "But when you have to turn into a chrysalis and then after that into a butterfly, I should think you'll feel it a little strange, won't you?"

"Not a bit," said the Caterpillar.

"Well, perhaps your feelings may be different," said Alice. "All I know is, it would feel very strange to me."

For some minutes the Caterpillar puffed away without speaking, but at last

it took the hookah out of its mouth again, and said, "So you think you're changed, do you? What size do you want to be?"

"Oh, I'm not particular as to size," Alice hastily replied. "Only one doesn't like changing so often, you know."

"I don't know," said the Caterpillar. Alice said nothing; she had never been so much contradicted in her life before, and she felt that she was losing her temper. "Are you content now?" said the caterpillar.

"Well, I should like to be a little larger, sir, if you wouldn't mind," said Alice. "Three inches is such a wretched height to be."

"It is a very good height indeed!" said the Caterpillar angrily, rearing itself upright as it spoke (it was exactly three inches high).

"But I'm not used to it!" pleaded poor Alice in a piteous tone.

"You'll get used to it in time," said the Caterpillar, and it put the hookah into its mouth and began smoking again.

This time Alice waited patiently. In a minute or two the Caterpillar got down off the mushroom, and crawled away in the grass, merely remarking as it went, "One side will make you grow taller, and the other side will make you grow shorter."

'One side of what? The other side of what?' thought Alice to herself.

"Of the mushroom," said the Caterpillar, just as if she had asked it aloud; and in another moment it was out of sight.

Alice looked thoughtfully at the mushroom for a minute, trying to make out which were the two sides of it. At last she stretched her arms round it as far as they would go, and broke off a bit of the edge with each hand.

'And now which is which?' she said to herself, and nibbled a little of the right-hand bit to try the effect. The next moment she was shrinking rapidly, so she set to work at once to eat some of the other bit.

It was so long since she had been anything near the right size that it felt quite strange at first; but she got used to it in a few minutes, and began talking to herself, as usual. 'There's half my plan done now! How puzzling all these changes are! However, I've got back to my right size. The next thing is to get into that beautiful garden—how is that to be done, I wonder?' As she said this, she came suddenly upon an open place, with a little house in it about four feet high. 'Whoever lives there,' thought Alice, 'it'll never do to come upon them this size. Why, I should frighten them out of their wits!' So she began nibbling at the right hand bit again and did not venture to go near the house till she had brought herself down to nine inches high.

Suddenly a footman in livery came running out of the wood—judging by his face only, she would have called him a fish—and rapped loudly at the door with his knuckles. It was opened by another foot-man in livery, with a round face and large eyes like a frog. Both footmen, Alice noticed, had powdered hair that curled all over their heads.

The Fish-Footman began by producing from under his arm a great letter, nearly as large as himself, saying in a solemn tone, "For the Duchess. An invitation from the Queen to play croquet." The Frog-Footman repeated, in the same solemn tone, only changing the order of the words a little, "From the Queen. An invitation for the Duchess to play croquet." Then they both bowed low, and their curls got entangled together.

Alice laughed so much at this that she had to run back into the wood for fear of their hearing her; when she next peeped out, the Fish-Footman was

gone, and the other was sitting on the ground near the door.

Alice went timidly up to the door and knocked. At this moment, the door of the house opened and a large plate came skimming out, straight at the Footman's head. It grazed his nose and broke to pieces against one of the trees behind him.

The door led right into a large kitchen, which was full of smoke from one end to the other. The Duchess was sitting on a three-legged stool in the middle, nursing a baby; the cook was leaning over the fire, stirring a cauldron full of soup.

'There's certainly too much pepper in that soup!' Alice said to herself, as well as she could for sneezing.

There was certainly too much of it in the air. Even the Duchess sneezed occasionally and as for the baby, it was sneezing and howling alternately without a moment's pause. The only things in the kitchen that did not sneeze were the cook and a large cat, which was sitting on the hearth and grinning from ear to ear.

"Would you tell me," asked Alice, "why your cat grins like that?"

"It's a Cheshire cat," said the Duchess.

"I didn't know that Cheshire cats always grinned; in fact, I didn't know that cats could grin," said Alice.

"You don't know much," said the Duchess, "and that's a fact."

Alice did not like the tone of this remark and thought it would be as well to introduce some other subject of conversation. While she was trying to fix on one, the cook took the cauldron of soup off the fire, and at once set to work throwing everything within her reach at the Duchess and the baby.

"Oh, please mind what you're doing!" cried Alice, jumping up and down in an agony of terror.

"Here! You may nurse it a bit, if you like!" the Duchess said to Alice, flinging the baby at her as she spoke. "I must go and get ready to play croquet with the Queen," and she hurried out of the room.

Alice caught the baby with some difficulty, as it was a queer-shaped little creature, and held out its arms and legs in all directions. The poor little thing was snorting like a steam-engine when she caught it, and kept doubling itself up and straightening itself out again, so that it was as much as she could do to hold it. The baby grunted, and Alice looked very anxiously into its face to see what was the matter with it. There could be no doubt that it had a very turned-up nose, much more like a snout than a real nose; also its eyes were extremely small for a baby. Alice did not like the look of the thing at all.

"If you're going to turn into a pig," said Alice seriously, "I'll have nothing more to do with you." The creature grunted again, so violently that she looked down into its face in some alarm. This time there could be no mistake about it: it was neither more nor less than a pig, so she set the little creature down and felt quite relieved to see it trot away quietly into the wood. 'If it had grown up,' she said to herself, 'it would have made a dreadfully ugly child. But it makes rather a handsome pig, I think.'

Alice looked up and was a little startled to see the Cheshire Cat sitting on a bough of a tree a few yards off. The Cat only grinned when it saw Alice. It looked good-natured, she thought. Still, it had very long claws and a great many teeth, so she felt that it ought to be treated with respect.

"Cheshire Puss," she began, rather timidly, as she did not at all know

whether it would like the name. "Would you tell me, please, which way I ought to go from here?"

"That depends a good deal on where you want to get to," said the Cat.

"I don't much care where—" said Alice.

"Then it doesn't matter which way you go," said the Cat.

"—so long as I get somewhere," Alice added as an explanation.

"Oh, you're sure to do that," said the Cat, "if you only walk long enough."

Alice felt that this could not be denied, so she tried another question. "What sort of people live here?"

"In that direction," the Cat said, waving its right paw round, "lives a Hatter. And in that direction," waving the other paw, "lives a March Hare. They're both mad."

"But I don't want to go among mad people," Alice remarked.

"Oh, you can't help that. We're all mad here." said the Cat, and vanished.

Alice was not much surprised at this. After a minute or two she walked on in the direction in which the March Hare was said to live.

She had not gone much farther before she came in sight of the house of the March Hare. She thought it must be the right house because the chimneys were shaped like ears and the roof was thatched with fur. There was a table set out under a tree in front of the house and the March Hare and the Hatter were having tea at it; a Dormouse was sitting between them, fast asleep. The table was a large one, but the three were all crowded together at one corner of it. "No room! No room!" they cried out when they saw Alice coming.

"There's plenty of room!" said Alice indignantly, and she sat down in a large chair at one end of the table.

The Hatter opened his eyes very wide on hearing this but all he said was, "Why is a raven like a writing-desk?"

"I believe I can guess that," said Alice.

"Do you mean that you think you can find out the answer to it?" said the March Hare.

"Exactly so," said Alice.

"Then you should say what you mean," the March Hare went on.

"I do," Alice hastily replied; "at least I mean what I say—that's the same thing."

"Not the same thing at all!" said the Hatter. "You might just as well say that 'I see what I eat' is the same thing as 'I eat what I see!'"

"You might just as well say," added the March Hare, "that 'I like what I get' is the same thing as 'I get what I like!'" Here the conversation dropped and the party sat silent for a minute while Alice thought over all she could remember about ravens and writing-desks, which wasn't much.

The Hatter was the first to break the silence. "What day of the month is it?" he said turning to Alice. He had taken his watch out of his pocket and was looking at it uneasily, shaking it every now and then, and holding it to his ear.

Alice considered a little, and then said, "The fourth."

"Two days wrong!" sighed the Hatter.

Alice had been looking over his shoulder with some curiosity. "What a funny watch!" she remarked. "It tells the day of the month and doesn't tell what o'clock it is!"

"Why should it?" muttered the Hatter. "Does your watch tell you what year it is?"

"Of course not," Alice replied. "But that's because it stays the same year for such a long time."

"Which is just the case with mine," said the Hatter.

Alice felt dreadfully puzzled. The Hatter's remark seemed to have no sort of meaning in it and yet it was certainly English. "I don't quite understand you," she said, as politely as she could.

"Have you guessed the riddle yet?" the Hatter said, turning to Alice again.

"No, I give it up," Alice replied. "What's the answer?"

"I haven't the slightest idea," said the Hatter.

Alice sighed wearily. "I think you might do something better with the time," she said, "than waste it in asking riddles that have no answers."

"If you knew Time as well as I do," said the Hatter, "you wouldn't talk about wasting it. It's him."

"I don't know what you mean," said Alice.

"Of course you don't!" the Hatter said. "I dare say you never even spoke to Time!"

"Perhaps not," Alice replied. "But I know I have to beat time when I learn music."

"Ah! That accounts for it," said the Hatter. "Now, if you only kept on good terms with him, he'd do almost anything you liked with the clock. For instance, suppose it were nine o'clock in the morning, just time to begin lessons. You'd only have to whisper a hint to Time and round goes the clock in a twinkling! Half-past one, time for dinner!"

"That would be grand, certainly," said Alice thoughtfully. "But then—I shouldn't be hungry for it, you know."

"Not at first, perhaps," said the Hatter. "But you could keep it to half-past one as long as you liked."

"Is that the way you manage?" Alice asked.

The Hatter shook his head mournfully. "Not I!" he replied. "We quarreled last March and ever since he won't do a thing I ask! It's always six o'clock now."

A bright idea came into Alice's head. "Is that the reason so many tea things are put out here?" she asked.

"Yes, that's it," said the Hatter with a sigh. "It's always tea time, and we've no time to wash the things between whiles."

"Then you keep moving round, I suppose?" said Alice.

"Exactly so," said the Hatter. "As the things get used up."

"But what happens when you come to the beginning again?" Alice ventured to ask.

"Suppose we change the subject," the March Hare interrupted, yawning. "Take some more tea," he said to Alice.

"I've had nothing yet," Alice replied in an offended tone, "so I can't take more."

"You mean you can't take less," said the Hatter. "It's very easy to take more than nothing."

Alice did not quite know what to say to this so she helped herself to some tea and bread and butter.

"I want a clean cup," interrupted the Hatter. "Let's all move one place on."

He moved on as he spoke and the Dormouse followed him. The March Hare moved into the Dormouse's place and Alice rather unwillingly took the place of the March Hare. The Hatter was the only one who got any advantage from the change and Alice was a good deal worse off than before, as the March Hare had just upset the milk jug into his plate.

This piece of rudeness was more than Alice could bear. She got up in disgust and walked off. "I'll never go there again!" said Alice as she picked her way through the wood. "It's the stupidest tea party I ever was at in all my life!"

Just as she said this, she noticed that one of the trees had a door leading right into it. 'That's very curious!' she thought. 'But everything's curious today. I think I may as well go in.' And in she went.

Once more she found herself in the long hall close to the little glass table. 'I'll manage better this time,' she said to herself, and began by taking the little golden key and unlocking the door that led into the garden. Then she nibbled at the mushroom (she had kept a piece of it in her pocket) till she was about a foot high. Then she walked down the little passage, and found herself at last in the beautiful garden.

A large rose tree stood near the entrance of the garden. The roses growing on it were white but there were three gardeners busily painting them red. Just as she came up to them she heard one of them say, "Look out now, Five! Don't go splashing paint over me like that!"

"You'd better not talk, Seven!" said Five. "I heard the Queen say only yesterday you deserved to be beheaded!"

Seven flung down his brush, and had just begun "Well, of all the unjust things—" when his eye chanced to fall upon Alice and he checked himself suddenly. The others looked round also, and all of them bowed low.

"Would you tell me," said Alice, a little timidly, "why you are painting those roses?"

Two began in a low voice, "Why you see, Miss, this here ought to have been a red rose tree. We put a white one in by mistake and if the Queen was to find out, we should all have our heads cut off." At this moment Five called out, "The Queen! The Queen!" and the three gardeners threw themselves flat upon their faces. There was a sound of many footsteps, and Alice looked round, eager to see the Queen.

First came ten soldiers carrying clubs; next ten courtiers ornamented all over with diamonds. After these came the royal children; there were ten of them, and they were all ornamented with hearts. Next came the guests and among them Alice recognized the White Rabbit. Last of all came the King and Queen of hearts.

When the procession came to Alice they all stopped and looked at her, and the Queen said severely, "What's your name, child?"

"My name is Alice," said Alice very politely; but she added, to herself, 'Why, they're only a pack of cards. I needn't be afraid of them!'

"Can you play croquet?" asked the Queen.

"Yes!" said Alice.

"Come on, then!" roared the Queen, and Alice joined the procession.

"It's a very fine day!" said a timid voice at her side. She was walking by the White Rabbit, who was peeping anxiously into her face.

"Very," said Alice. "Where's the Duchess?"

"Hush!" said the Rabbit in a low, hurried tone. He looked anxiously over his shoulder as he spoke, and then raised himself upon tiptoe, put his mouth close to her ear, and whispered, "She's under sentence of execution."

"Get to your places!" shouted the Queen in a voice of thunder and people

began running about in all directions; they got settled down in a minute or two, and the game began. Alice thought she had never seen such a curious croquet-ground in her life; the balls were live hedgehogs, the mallets live flamingoes, and the soldiers had to double themselves up and stand on their hands and feet to make the arches.

The chief difficulty Alice found at first was in managing her flamingo. She succeeded in getting its body tucked away under her arm, with its legs hanging down. But just as she had got its neck nicely straightened out, and was going to give the hedgehog a blow with its head, it would twist itself round and look up in her face, with such a puzzled expression that she could not help bursting out laughing. And when she had got its head down, and was going to begin again, she found that the hedgehog had unrolled itself, and was in the act of crawling away. The players all played at once without waiting for turns, and in a very short time the Queen was in a furious passion and went stamping about, shouting, 'Off with his head!' or 'Off with her head!' about once in a minute.

Alice began to feel very uneasy. She had not as yet had any dispute with the Queen, but she knew that it might happen at any minute. 'They're dreadfully fond of beheading people here,' thought Alice. 'The great wonder is, that there's anyone left alive!'

She was looking about for some way of escape, and wondering whether she could get away without being seen, when she noticed a curious appearance in the air. She made it out to be a grin, and she said to herself 'It's the Cheshire Cat.'

"How do you like the queen?" said the Cat, as soon as there was mouth enough for it to speak with.

"Not at all," said Alice. "She's so extremely—" Just then she noticed that the Queen was close behind her, listening. So she went on, "—likely to win, that it's hardly worth while finishing the game."

The Queen smiled and passed on.

"Who are you talking to?" said the King, going up to Alice, and looking at the Cat with great curiosity.

"It's a friend of mine—a Cheshire Cat," said Alice. "Allow me to introduce it."

"I don't like the look of it at all. It must be removed," said the King very decidedly, and he called the Queen, who was passing at the moment. "My dear! I wish you would have this cat removed!"

The Queen had only one way of settling all difficulties, great or small. "Off with his head!" she said, without even looking around.

"I'll fetch the executioner myself," said the King eagerly, and he hurried off.

Alice thought she might as well go back and see how the game was going on, so she went in search of her hedgehog. When she got back to the Cheshire Cat, she was surprised to find quite a large crowd collected round it. There was a dispute going on between the executioner, the King, and the Queen, who were all talking at once.

The moment Alice appeared, she was appealed to by all three to settle the question, and they repeated their arguments to her. Alice could think of nothing else to say but "It belongs to the Duchess, you'd better ask her about it."

"She's in prison," the Queen said to the executioner. "Fetch her here." And the executioner went off like an arrow.

The Cat's head began fading away the moment he was gone, and, by the

time he had come back with the Duchess, it had entirely disappeared; so the King and the executioner ran wildly up and down looking for it, while the rest of the party went back to the game.

"You can't think how glad I am to see you again!" said the Duchess, as she tucked her arm into Alice's and they walked off together.

Alice was very glad to find her in such a pleasant temper. "The game's going rather better now," she said, by way of keeping up the conversation a little.

" 'Tis so," said the Duchess, "and the moral of that is—'tis love, 'tis love, that makes the world go round!'"

"Somebody said," Alice whispered, "that it's done by everybody minding their own business!"

"Ah, well! It means much the same thing," said the Duchess as she added, "and the mora—"

But here, to Alice's great surprise, the Duchess's voice died away in the middle of her favorite word 'moral,' and the arm that was linked into hers began to tremble. Alice looked up, and there stood the Queen in front of them.

"A fine day, your Majesty!" the Duchess began in a low, weak voice.

"I give you fair warning," shouted the Queen, stamping on the ground as she spoke. "Either you or your head must be off! Take your choice!"

The Duchess took her choice and was gone in a moment.

"Let's go on with the game," the Queen said to Alice, and Alice was too much frightened to say a word, but slowly followed her back to the croquet-ground.

All the time they were playing, the Queen never left off quarrelling with the other players and shouting "Off with his head!" or "Off with her head!" Those whom she sentenced were taken into custody by the soldiers who, of course, had to leave off being arches to do this, so that by the end of half an hour there were no arches left, and all the players, except the King, the Queen, and Alice, were in custody and under sentence of execution.

Then the Queen said to Alice, "Have you seen the Mock Turtle yet?"

"No," said Alice. "I don't even know what a Mock Turtle is."

"Come on, then," said the Queen, "and he shall tell you his history."

They very soon came upon a Gryphon, lying fast asleep in the sun.

"Up, lazy thing!" said the Queen, "and take this young lady to see the Mock Turtle, and to hear his history. I must go back and see after some executions I have ordered," and she walked off, leaving Alice alone with the Gryphon.

The Gryphon sat up and rubbed its eyes. It watched the Queen till she was out of sight, then it chuckled. "What fun!" said the Gryphon.

"What is the fun?" asked Alice.

"Why, it's all her fancy," said the Gryphon. "They never execute anybody, you know. Come on!"

So they went up to the Mock Turtle, who looked at them with large eyes full of tears, but said nothing.

"This here young lady," said the Gryphon, "she wants to know your history, she do."

"I'll tell it her," said the Mock Turtle in a deep, hollow tone. "Sit down, both of you, and don't speak a word till I've finished."

"Once," said the Mock Turtle with a deep sigh, "I was a real Turtle. When

we were little, we went to school in the sea. The master was an old Turtle—we used to call him Tortoise—"

"Why did you call him Tortoise, if he wasn't one?" Alice asked.

"We called him Tortoise because he taught us," said the Mock Turtle angrily. "Really, you are very dull!" And he went on: "Yes, we went to school in the sea, though you mayn't believe it—"

"I never said I didn't!" interrupted Alice.

"You did," said the Mock Turtle. "We had the best of educations—in fact, we went to school every day—"

"And how many hours a day did you do lessons?" said Alice.

"Ten hours the first day," said the Mock Turtle. "Nine the next, and so on."

"What a curious plan!" exclaimed Alice.

This was quite a new idea to Alice, and she thought it over a little before she made her next remark. "Then the eleventh day must have been a holiday."

"Of course it was," said the Mock Turtle.

"And how did you manage on the twelfth?" Alice went on eagerly.

"That's enough about lessons," the Gryphon interrupted in a very decided tone.

"Oh, a song, please, if the Mock Turtle would be so kind," Alice replied, so eagerly that the Gryphon said, "Sing her "Turtle Soup," will you, old fellow?"

The Mock Turtle sighed deeply, and began to sing this:

"Beautiful Soup, so rich and green,

Waiting in a hot tureen!

Who for such dainties would not stoop?

Soup of the evening, beautiful Soup!

Soup of the evening, beautiful Soup!

Beau—ootiful Soo—oop!

Beau—ootiful Soo—oop!

Soo—oop of the e—e—evening,

Beautiful, beautiful Soup!

"Chorus again!" cried the Gryphon, and the Mock Turtle had just begun to repeat it, when a cry of "The trial's beginning!" was heard in the distance.

"Come on!" cried the Gryphon, and taking Alice by the hand, it hurried off, without waiting for the end of the song.

"What trial is it?" Alice panted as she ran; but the Gryphon only answered "Come on!" and ran faster.

The King and Queen of Hearts were seated on their thrones when they arrived. A great crowd was assembled about them and the Knave was standing before them, in chains, with a soldier on each side to guard him. Near the King was the White Rabbit, with a trumpet in one hand, and a scroll of parchment in the other. In the very middle of the court was a table, with a large dish of tarts upon it. They looked so good that it made Alice quite hungry to look at them. 'I wish they'd get the trial done,' she thought, 'and hand round the refreshments!' But there seemed to be no chance of this, so she began looking at everything about her to pass the time.

The judge was the King. The twelve jurors were all writing very busily on slates.

"Herald, read the accusation!" said the King.

The White Rabbit blew three blasts on the trumpet and then unrolled the parchment scroll and read as follows:

"The Queen of Hearts, she made some tarts,

All on a summer day.

The Knave of Hearts, he stole those tarts,

And took them quite away!"

"Call the first witness," said the King and the White Rabbit blew three blasts on the trumpet and called out, "First witness!"

The first witness was the Hatter. He came in with a teacup in one hand and a piece of bread and butter in the other. "I beg pardon, your Majesty," he began, "for bringing these in but I hadn't quite finished my tea when I was sent for."

"Give your evidence," said the King "and don't be nervous, or I'll have you executed on the spot."

This did not seem to encourage the witness at all. He kept shift-ing from one foot to the other looking uneasily at the Queen. In his confusion, he bit a large piece out of his teacup instead of the bread and butter.

Just at this moment Alice felt a very curious sensation. She was beginning to grow larger again, and she thought at first she would get up and leave the court but on second thoughts she decided to remain where she was as long as there was room for her.

"Give your evidence," the King repeated angrily, "or I'll have you exe-cuted, whether you're nervous or not."

The miserable Hatter dropped his teacup and bread and butter and went down on one knee. "I'm a poor man, your Majesty," he began.

"You're a very poor speaker," said the King. "If that's all you know about it, you may stand down."

"I can't go no lower," said the Hatter. "I'm on the floor, as it is."

"You may go," said the King and the Hatter hurriedly left the court.

"Call the next witness!" said the King.

Alice watched the White Rabbit as he fumbled over the list, feeling very curious to see what the next witness would be like, '—for they haven't got much evidence yet,' she said to herself. Imagine her surprise, when the White Rabbit read out, at the top of his shrill little voice, the name "Alice!"

"Here!" cried Alice.

"What do you know about this business?" the King said to Alice.

"Nothing," said Alice.

At this moment the King, who had been busily writing in his notebook, cackled out "Silence!" and read out from his book, "Rule Forty-two. All persons more than a mile high must leave the court."

Everybody looked at Alice.

"That's not a regular rule. You invented it just now," said Alice.

"It's the oldest rule in the book," said the King.

"Then it ought to be Number One," said Alice.

"Off with her head!" the Queen shouted at the top of her voice.

"Who cares for you?" said Alice (she had grown to her full size by this time). "You're nothing but a pack of cards!"

At this the whole pack rose up into the air, and came flying down upon her. She tried to beat them off, and found herself lying on her back, with her head in the lap of her sister, who was gently brushing away some dead leaves that had fluttered down from the trees upon her face.

"Wake up, Alice dear!" said her sister. "Why, what a long sleep you've had!"

"Oh, I've had such a curious dream!" said Alice. She told her sister, as well as she could remember, all these strange Adventures of hers that you have just been reading about, and when she had finished, her sister kissed her, and said, "It was a curious dream, dear, certainly, but now run in to your tea; it's getting late." So Alice got up and ran off, thinking while she ran, as well she might, what a wonderful dream it had been.

THE END